The Inner Wall

The Inner Wall

A NOVEL

DEBORAH PETTICORD

MOUNTAIN ARBOR
PRESS

MOUNTAIN ARBOR
PRESS

Alpharetta, Georgia

ISBN: 978-1-6653-0821-2 - Paperback
eISBN: 978-1-6653-0822-9 - eBook

Library of Congress Control Number: 2024907661

⊗This paper meets the requirements of ANSI/NISO Z39.48-1992 (Permanence of Paper)

Scripture quotations marked "NRSV" are from the New Revised Standard Version Bible, copyright © 1989 the Division of Christian Education of the National Council of the Churches of Christ in the United States of America. Used by permission. All rights reserved.

052924

The City, 1890

TWO BODIES HUNG from the upper span of the new bridge, hovering like ghosts in the fog. The groaning of the ropes was the only sound, even the birds were quiet. Slowly, a crowd of early risers gathered. They peeked from buggies, delivery carts and produce wagons. As they tried to make out the features of the unfortunate couple, their hushed voices were barely audible on the breeze.

The baker and the driver of the milk wagon were there. A farmer with a load of melons had stopped alongside them. They recognized the bodies of their customers—the young Chinese storekeeper and his Black wife—even though their faces were swollen, their hair matted and clothing soggy from the rain. No more than fourteen people were on the bridge, yet the news would travel fast.

One hundred feet below, the muddy river was swollen

from the previous night's storm with a few logs tumbling in the churning water. In contrast to the cold steel bridge with its bodies and the hungry river below, the riverbanks were thick with leafy-green saplings bobbing in a light wind, their slender trunks woven with honeysuckle vines. The sun began to rise over the low, blue mountains, staining the fog that surrounded the scene a troubling shade of vermillion.

CHAPTER ONE

The City, 1995

A MAN CLAMBERED down from the roof with a splintered remnant of slate and returned to his truck. It was the first of many shards to be hauled away from one of the oldest houses on Mission Ridge. Listed on the National Register and considered locally significant, it was custom built for a well-known surgeon, the first to live in the area after the native removal and the War between the States.

As the sun beat down on the hedges and the pungent smell of English boxwood lifted on the steamy air, Madeline Bowers rallied from her daydream on the veranda. She needed to search through the file one more time, to look for any historic documentation among the old records that would help define the materials she could use for home reparations. Finding artisans who still produced exceptionally classic materials would be a challenge, she knew.

A tile supplier in Atlanta would replace the vintage

slate. Maddie and her husband Russell, owners of the house, were certain this was the original roof. Now, over one hundred years later, there would be a new roof.

The slate they had chosen was beautiful, although this metamorphic rock derived from its sedimentary cousin, shale, would be costly. Its low water absorption made it resistant to damage from frost and freezing. Fire resistant and energy efficient, it came in shades of gray to black, green, red, purple, and brown—the color often determined by the amount of iron and organic material present in the rock. From the purple slate of North Wales to the black slate of Germany's Moselle and Rhine River valleys, its alluring qualities never failed to create a demand among the developers of luxury properties. The new slate would come from eastern Pennsylvania, a source much closer to home.

Maddie knew one thing her clients could count on in this part of the country was the ever-high humidity. When combined with a broad temperature range, any number of uncomfortable environments could be achieved. She lifted the collar of her blouse to pull the garment away from the perspiration rolling down her back and turned to go inside.

In a temperamental burst of power, the red-faced driver revved the bucket truck and repositioned it under a steep gable so the ridge tiles could be examined, leaving huge ruts in the side yard. The structure itself seemed to grimace.

It was a moody house, clutched by evergreens and ancient oaks, peering from the far edge of a bright sweep of lawn. An early Italian Renaissance Revival style, it had only a few details from the federal period, and its paired Ionic columns and large Palladian windows did nothing to brighten its presence. The window trim was painted in deep green and gray. The taupe façade attempted hospitality and failed.

In truth, she was beginning to regret the purchase, but Russell had been completely infatuated by the property. Keeping the home updated would fall to her. As an architect, she knew about materials, fixtures and finishes, and Russell could go back to the university classroom, secure in the knowledge that Maddie would find the solutions to keep the house standing for another century. While she was flattered by his confidence, the task was daunting. It was a real project, all right. There were so many things to do, details to oversee and this was only the beginning.

When the renovations were finished, they would need some new furniture. Many of Maddie's furnishings leaned to the contemporary side, but Russell loved all things ancient. He had installed his collection of antique, hand-painted tiles from around the world in the library, along with old prints of French cathedrals, Iberian villages, and Scottish farm scenes. The home was an incognizant dream for him. Their house on a hillside in the north shore neighborhood had been a practical investment, but this was an adventure in the making.

Engrossed in the details of the property contained in the file, Maddie barely heard the knock. Not waiting for the door to be opened, a tall woman with a bob of steel-gray hair came through. Zee Lunsford floated in, trailed by her granddaughter Vivienne, a leggy eleven-year-old with a fondness for fashion. The dog didn't even bark.

"Good morning, Maddie! When do they start on the roof?" asked Zee, pulling at a strand of lint on Vivienne's black scarf. Why did this child have to wear these things in such hot weather? Zee seldomly questioned Vivienne openly on matters of personal style. She felt that self-expression was constructive to emotional development, so she didn't often fuss over trivial apparel choices; however, the heat was irritating.

Her client for the day had cancelled and she couldn't say she was sorry. The tiresome hoarder no one could live with had been coming to therapy for years with no intention of confronting his problems. She was certain he continued just to torture her.

She had spent a long career helping people sort out their thorny troubles and was prone to drifting deeply into the analytical work of the therapist, but today she needed a break. Her neighbor's roof was a welcome distraction. Insistently, Zee asked again.

"When, did you say?"

"Hello, Zee," Maddie said, absently. "Next week, I hope. I have other projects to work on. You've probably heard about the new boutique hotel on the bluff near the museum? We actually won the bid! It's been approved for phase one."

The plan had been—and would continue to be—particularly challenging to keep within budget because of its precarious placement on the edge of the bluff, in the city's historic district. It was the spot the owners wanted—taking full advantage of the view. Typically, officials had been unhurried in granting permits, and Maddie was anxious to get started. So anxious that she hired an additional project manager to support the ordinary work of the firm, while her chief design team would attend to the John Allen, the name of the new establishment.

Maddie thought about the changes she had seen over the past twenty years. When she started her tiny company, empty riverfront warehouses were still standing. A few smokestacks still rose mysteriously from desolate parking lots, strewn with broken glass.

Now it seemed the riverfront had a life of its own and — *metaphorically speaking* — it was on fire! The historic district preservation organizations had gobbled blocks of the lower streets beneath the bluff in what had once been a flood zone — a problem now under control because of substantial investment in flood prevention and storm-water drainage.

With the help of large numbers of immigrant laborers during the late nineteenth century, many of the streets had been filled and raised as much as fourteen feet and additional levels had been added to the warehouses. A steadily constructed wall began where the rocky outcropping of the bluff receded and sank deep into the diaphragm of the city as it grew from the riverbank, across the narrow end of the valley and up Mission Ridge. It stabilized the side of the ridge, and the roadbed created a crowning edge for over a mile. It was over this backdrop that new development was taking shape. There were modern projects springing up in the area and Maddie's designers were up to their eyeballs in work. She barely finished one meeting before it was time to go into another. At the week's end she still needed a day or two to complete its tasks.

Tomorrow, a site conference was scheduled for a new riverfront restaurant and music hall and later, Maddie was to consult with installers about the challenging staircase at one of the firm's most recent projects — a repurposed manufacturing facility known as the Wheelhouse. Her thoughts were disrupted by the sound of rattling glassine sleeves.

Across the room and away from the vigilant eye of her grandmother, Vivienne was shuffling through a stack of old photographs from the box where Maddie's papers had been stored. She looked small against the floor-to-ceiling bookshelves, her attention given over completely to the images. Maddie's terrier, Bonnet, named for the well-placed patch of dark fur on the top of her head, had discovered the dangling black scarf and was springing straight up into the air to grasp the fringe, again and again. Undisturbed, Vivienne studied the photos.

There were early shots of the house. A carriage with a man and woman standing alongside, and a photo composed from down the street showing the high stone wall that helped support the side of the ridge and the roadway above. The surgeon's new house appeared in the background. There were even one or two construction photos.

"Who are *they*?" Vivienne asked her grandmother. The girl waved a black-and-white print of a group of men, a few with small and brimless round hats, most with long braids draped over broad shoulders.

"Viv, don't be so nosey," Zee chided before eagerly examining the photo.

"The clothes are kind of boring, but I wish I had one of those hats," Vivienne added.

Maddie crossed the room to peer over Zee's shoulder.

"A work crew, maybe?" Maddie offered. "That's the city wall behind them. Although . . . I don't remember seeing this photo—you found it here?"

Without waiting for her answer, Maddie turned the photo over and noticed a list of names and dates scrawled onto its yellowed back.

CHAN YEE, FOREMAN, 1888
SAM WAH, LABORER, 1889
CHAN OCK, LABORER, 1889

"Thank you, Vivienne," said Maddie. "This will add depth to the story of the house, and you know, every house has a story."

CHAPTER TWO

1890

Chan Yee

CHAN YEE WAITED three hours to receive the bodies of Sam and Ida Wah once they had been hauled down from the bridge. After a stern rebuke from the police chief, James Ottinger, the morgue had released them. It was difficult to look at the bodies, so different from the vibrant, attractive people they had been the day before.

Because Ida's family was scattered, they would both be buried according to Chinese custom. Ida was the daughter of an African slave, but hanging a woman was rare. He was stunned. Maybe, Chan Yee thought, he should ask the Christian pastor from the church they attended to pray over them, as well.

Chan Yee smoothed his woolen coat and straightened his fedora. He could feel his queue against his neck, extending down his back underneath the coat. Even though he had spent years laying heavy stone and his hands showed the wear, he still appeared youthful. He was fastidious in his habits and grooming. He had adapted to this new culture relatively quickly.

After the inner wall of the city had been finished, along with a few related construction projects, there was nothing left for the Chinese builders—Celestials, the locals called them. The term was a clumsy Western version of the ancient Chinese name "Tian Chao" which roughly translated to "Empire of Heaven."

Some of them left for New Orleans. Some opened vegetable markets or dry-goods stores. Chan Yee had opened a laundry on Sixth Street. Those who remained fostered an industrious, frugal, and unapologetic community with its own customs.

The undertaker had returned all of Sam and Ida's belongings with their bodies, save for some opium that they were reported to have hidden in their clothes. Chan Yee knew Americans were always upset by opium. For reasons he didn't understand, they could not quit wanting it once they took up the pipe. Maybe it was not a spiritual experience for them.

Occasionally, a few Chinese workers would gather to smoke and play cards in the upper room of a warehouse two doors down from Chan Yee's shop. Once or twice, he had seen Chief Ottinger and a couple of the other police officers raid the warehouse, mostly scattering the party. But Sam Wah had never been among them. He and Ida kept to themselves, operating a small market that sold tins of fish and tobacco to the Black community. Chan Yee was bewildered.

The door of the small wooden house near the docks on River Street was decorated with a white banner. The Wahs had shared the house with Sam's cousin, Chan Ock, who lived in a room off the back porch. A few mourners were waiting outside to join the funeral procession. Inside, a dozen guests had come to pay their respects. A table was laid with rice cakes and dried fish, pickled eggs, and other delights the deceased might want in the next life. A clutch of white lilies in a jar had been placed beside the small tintype photograph of the young couple. In the picture, they were wearing their best clothes in stone-faced silence. Two rough, pine coffins draped in white cloths sat on blocks near the table.

In the city, Sam and Ida had fewer family members than friends available to mourn. Most were neighbors and store customers. A line extended from the front door to around the parlor, where Chan Ock and other community members took their turns, some bowing before the bodies three times each.

Even though he now attended the New Monumental Christian Church, Chan Yee read the Buddhist passages aloud from his mother's prayer book. She had given it to him when he left his home province years before and he often found it comforting when he was sad and confused, as he was now.

"May the powerless find power. May those in the fearful wilderness be guarded by beneficent celestials. May all beings awaken to their true nature and be free." It was an all-encompassing prayer, yet simple.

Carefully, eight men from Sam's former work crew loaded the coffins into the rented hearse pulled by a team of mules. The small entourage followed, most of them clad in long white shirts or tunics, as another mourner struck a brass symbol with a small mallet. It rang, shrilly, all the way to Pleasant Garden Cemetery at the base of Mission Ridge.

The old cemetery was crowded with the graves of former African slaves, about a third of whom had died from disease. The yellow fever epidemic of 1878 had caused the deaths of over three hundred people in the city, including a few refugees from the Mississippi River basin, where the fever seemed to originate.

More than ninety percent of Whites living in Memphis had contracted yellow fever when it swept through, and roughly seventy percent of them died. Former slaves suffered from the fever in large numbers as well, although only seven percent of infected Blacks died. There was no consensus among the medical experts to explain the racial disparity in mortality rates, yet repeated exposure to yellow fever over many generations in West Africa may have provided the African descendants with a higher resistance to the disease.

Still, the fever had killed many of the city's Black folk, and Pleasant Garden Cemetery was already almost full. These newly received caskets would be relegated to a fringe of unimproved ground at the very back. Two Black congregations in the city shared this ground. They would not have been allowed to rest in Pleasant Garden at all had Ida not been part of the New Monumental congregation. Sam had been gradually becoming a member, the way many Chinese immigrants were slowly becoming westernized.

Their headstones were simple white markers laid flat and engraved with the date and the Chinese characters for Wah. Once the mourners were gathered at the gravesite, pieces of gold paper were burned, the smoke blew back into the faces of the attendees. It was traditional, ghost money, to be used in the afterlife. Chan Yee poured out a goblet of wine near the graves. In doing so, according to the Chinese among them, they were ready to be received in paradise.

The current minister of the New Monumental Church, Reverend Frederick Thirkill, who was himself a former slave, took up the proceedings with a booming voice that howled out the twenty-third Psalm with stinging clarity and irrefutable authority. Ida's cousin Mae and one of her friends sang a new hymn called "Deep River," something she heard at a church in Atlanta.

> *Oh, don't you want to go,*
> *To the Gospel feast,*
> *That Promised Land,*
> *Where all is peace?*
> *Oh, deep river, Lord,*
> *I want to cross over into campground.*

It was a slow and lamenting duet under a blue sky. In the rising heat of the day the smell of shortleaf pine mingled with incense. All the while, a trio of paid Chinese mourners wailed in the background. It was an extra expense, some would say even extravagant, but he wanted the ceremony to be correct.

High above, a red-tailed hawk screamed as it flew from its nest, and the wall of stone produced a chilling echo of sounds.

A shiver ran up Chan Yee's neck. He had been the foreman of Sam's work crew and his friend. He had handled the funeral arrangements, but he was doubtful there would be any justice.

He remembered the day he first met Sam.

Seven men stood waiting near a stack of crates which were filled with assorted dry goods and utensils. The men had been assigned to Chan Yee, who gave each of them a blanket, a cup, a spoon, and a plate. He wrote down their names and then spoke to them in Mandarin and in English. He told them they would take the first section of the north wall and would be expected to finish it in six weeks.

"Finishing on time will make all the difference because you will want to be paid on time," he explained. A couple of the men still looked confused, so he addressed them in another dialect, until finally an expression of understanding, then relief, appeared on their faces. Chan Yee observed other groups of men around the compound. Some crews numbered as many as ten.

The supervisor came around eventually. He was a big man who didn't like questions.

"Could we get one or two more workmen?" he asked the construction manager.

"Not likely," growled the burly man. "When we built the last dock warehouse, we never had enough of them and most of the lot were troublemakers." He picked up the roster in his beefy hands and counted the crew on the list of incomprehensible names.

"Let's hope these men are better."

"Why would they be?" He growled. "We have miles of wall to build, and they'll be twisting my arm to stay on schedule. But if anybody else shows up, I'll send 'em your way." He turned and walked with steady resolve toward another crew member.

A rundown remnant of an army barracks and a few tents would be their quarters until something better could be constructed and after the crew had settled in, Chan Yee put a kettle of water to boil over his fire. He hadn't yet warmed to the idea of coffee, and this pot of tea was the last of his supply from home.

"Excuse me," said a voice from behind him. He turned

and saw a slender Chinese man who was smiling, and re-markably, speaking to him in English. "My name is Sam Wah. I was told to ask you about work."

Chan Yee looked at him and thought to himself how frail the man appeared to be—and taking on such heavy labor. He gave it a mental shrug. "Would you like a cup of tea?"

CHAPTER THREE

1995
Maddie

THIS WAS THE eve of the annual lecture, so Maddie wrapped up the final file for the application for historic renovation, thinking about the details of the project. She had hoped Russell would become more directly involved with the process, but his way of helping was apparently purely visionary. It wasn't that he didn't want to be helpful, he just wasn't sure how.

She had to agree with all his friends, Russell Bowers had enjoyed the best of everything, including an arguably privileged upbringing. He was the son of an educator who married the daughter of a wealthy manufacturer. While his good fortune could have caused jealousy, no one begrudged him anything. Possessing a charismatic smile, the ruddy good looks of a white man aging gracefully, and an easygoing temperament, he was fondly known throughout his community.

Maddie was gazing out over the valley from the large window of their drawing room when Russell came home. He wrapped his arms around her, and they stood there watching. The river sparkled beneath the late evening sky, the bank on the far side a terrace of festive lights, just coming on. The bridge rose against the horizon, dominating the dusky landscape. A riverboat passed underneath, throbbing with music, flashing like a fairground.

She felt him withdraw because scenes like these never failed to send his thoughts back in time, before bridges or riverboats, when history was unwritten. She knew he was preparing for his symposium presentation. It would be open to the community as always, and she would attend as she always did.

The next evening Maddie hurried up the steps and through the heavy wooden door. The historic building—one of the oldest on campus—held a modern lecture hall with high-tech amenities. She found a comfortable spot near the rear and heard Russell say, *Everything began at the riverbank.*" Then he began describing the lives of Archaic people in an animated and empathetic way.

"These riverbanks have been a center of life for millennia. Paleo-Indian hunters moved through the land as receding glaciers sculpted the Ohio and Tennessee River Valleys. Over time, as climate became more hospitable, the descendants of these hunters—the Archaic people—began to establish more permanent settlements in the region. These small clans grew progressively larger and the competition for resources increased. They began to fight each other in lean years of pestilence or drought. Eventually, the clans outgrew the protection of caves. With their populations increasing, the tribes began to build huts and palisades in villages nearer to the banks of the great river.

"We are separated from these people by thousands of years. Caves and mounds are what we have left of them, our only way to reach them."

With the aid of photographs of the simple tools and earth mounds still in existence, Russell illustrated their lives. They evolved into the Woodland, then Mississippian tribal people who inhabited the river valleys. Generations of them had been born, lived, and died—leaving giant burial mounds, pottery shards, clam shells, ornaments, and simple tools.

"These were the mound builders, and their numbers grew dramatically throughout the southeast. Their bustling towns became centers of commerce fueled by agriculture. They were part of the greater Coosa Chiefdom, which was invaded by Hernando de Soto and an army of Spaniards. His men had no intention of establishing permanent settlements, but the Old World diseases they brought with them decimated the native populations."

The next series of slides showed exotic rainforests, Incan clothes and artifacts made of gold. He reminded listeners that the Gold Museum in Bogota, Columbia, was dedicated to a huge collection, over thirty-four thousand pieces of pre-Hispanic, gold artifacts. Maddie noticed that across the lecture hall, this series drew more attention than pottery shards and arrowheads.

Bringing the focus back home, Russell reminded listeners that the day Soto marched into the Mission Ridge area looking for gold, he discovered Citico Town and the mound at its center, near the mouth of Citico Creek, between the ridge and the river.

"The Citico Mound has been systematically demolished to make way for twentieth-century highway projects. The site was second in size only to the great southern mounds at Etowah, but its artifacts were pilfered over the years. Little evidence was left of the culture, or of the Spaniards' exploratory invasion.

"When the Cherokee leader Nancy Ward, and later the defiant Dragging Canoe, came on the scene their people were living on small farms in the five remaining Cherokee towns along the river. The river was the artery of the region, creating transportation routes, allowing commerce. Yet, settling this wild and expansive region and preparing it for agricultural pursuits required backbreaking work. Others were brought in to do that work—African slaves—even before the tribes were sent away.

"The mountainous region around the Cherokee towns was not ideal for large plantations, yet south of the great river the land opened up for agriculture, especially after the native removal in 1838. The removal took place years after the death of Nancy Ward, who had dreamed repeatedly in her later life of a long line of her people marching west, leaving corpses along the way. The "real people," as they called themselves, were rounded up and forced to leave from Blythe's Ferry and Ross' Landing. Four thousand died on the way to the Oklahoma territory.

"Life along the riverbank began to look slightly different."

At this point, most of the one-hundred-fifty attendees rose at Russell's encouragement and stretched for an intermission. Most were university alums. The swell of soft conversation filled the theater. Maddie spoke to several old friends who made sure she saw them and received their compliments to her husband. She maneuvered toward the coffee kiosk with a little time to down a half a cup before the lights flashed twice and the crowd returned to their seats.

"On July 29, 1839, an enslaved man named Jacob Cummings took an old Indian canoe and pushed off from the shores of Moccasin Bend near the ferry crossing. He crossed to Williams Island, where he camped for a day or two, then swam across at a narrow neck of the river to the north shore, farther upstream. Working his way upland and traveling mostly at night, he navigated the Underground Railroad, first crossing the Ohio River into Indiana and finally going all the way to Canada. He later became an agent and leader of a community of runaways on the Puce River in Ontario, helping many more people find a place to be free and live productively. The communities of freemen remained intact until the war for emancipation began.

"Four long years of conflict and horror tested the union of the states and the will of people collectively to survive the destruction and rebuild their economies.

"After the bloody war, Chinese immigrants came, only welcome as replacements for the slaves—a temporary fix that proved too costly. But for a time the Chinese built walls, laid tracks for the rail lines, and carved out roadways for low wages. Then, they ran dry goods stores and laundering services. Most of them eventually returned home to China or moved to larger cities where their ethnic communities were more culturally significant and jobs more plentiful. Slowly, the city on the banks of the river grew, adding a hospital and a university."

At this point he introduced the newly discovered images of the Chinese work crew from the construction of his own home.

"The story does not end here," Russell brought the presentation to a close. "What little remains of the Chinese immigrant culture here is difficult to find, and its contribution to the region is a point of speculation, but it is important to acknowledge all the players."

Maddie was sure the applause was gratifying to Russell. Sometimes these academic things could be stuffy, yet she thought her husband always brought the people he was discussing to scale and made them incredibly alive.

After the presentation they strolled with friends down the street to a favorite rooftop bar. The night sky was filled with stars, and they settled into a pleasant conversation.

"This area has seen so many amazing cultural and climactic changes," Russell offered as he adjusted his pace to match the others.

"You know, I thought I knew the history of this town, but where did you come up with those photographs of Chinese builders? Am I supposed to suspend my disbelief that they're even real?" said one of Russell's colleagues.

"Of course, they're real," said Maddie. "We found them in the historic documents and papers for the house. Luckily someone saved them." Maddie suspected Russell would come to obsess over the new information.

"I was glad I was able to include the photographs, but I only wish we knew more about those workers and their lives," mused Russell. He thought about Chan Yee and Sam Wah and what life must have been like for them as they worked on the house.

CHAPTER FOUR

1883

Chan Yee

CHAN YEE HIMSELF had arrived in the spring. From the Port of New Orleans, he had taken passage on a steam-powered riverboat that churned its way upriver to Memphis. From there, an east-bound coach took him first to Nashville, and then to the city, where he reported to his recruiters. He was assigned a bunk and given a few essential items.

He waited in line for his first meal at the cook tent. Carrying the tin tray to a table where eleven other men were eating, he looked at the strange food. Soon he would grow familiar with the hunk of cornbread, field peas and turnip greens with a little pork fat that constituted almost every evening meal. A cook with dirty hands ladled grits out for breakfast and lunch too, when there was time. Chan Yee longed for rice, yet was thankful for the regularity of the meals, because the work was hard.

The limestone for the wall came from the Stone Fort quarry a few miles downriver. It was loaded onto flatbed wagons that were driven up the ridge, pulled by mule teams.

If the men worked hard, the mules worked even harder. The team of sixteen mules was led by a pair named Billie and Doc, a handsome team of red mules brought all the way from Missouri. With feet as big as supper plates, they would make it possible to build the wall.

The mules were smart and sensible about the track and its elevation—in fact, for this work, they were superior to horses in every way, Chan Yee observed.

The wheeler and the swamper were two riders who stayed close to the wagons. The wheeler rode the horse on the left and drove the team with a long rein, known as a jerk line. The second man, the swamper, rode at the back of the trailer to operate the brake during steep descents. They were responsible for readying the team, feeding and watering the mules, and providing any veterinary care or wagon repairs that needed to be done.

Fresh mules and fresh men were always sought after. The work was intense, and the need was exacerbated during the late summer months when the heat and humidity reached record levels during the first year. The atmosphere created a tension and irritability among the work crews. They tried, eventually without success, to force themselves to ignore the growing irritation.

One August day, two men in Chan Yee's work crew got into an argument over an iron chisel they were using to fit the limestone blocks into ordered rows along the wall. For days they had been lashing out at each other, each goading and defiant. Their disputes ran deep, as they were brothers with a competitive history. They were even in love with the same woman back home. A woman from another social class who neither could marry. The gang had heard the story.

Zhang Wei and his brother Zhang Yong were true to their given names. One was big and the other was brave. Zhang Wei was trying to position a stone in the wall and needed to chip off a jagged edge when he reached for the iron chisel. At exactly that time, Zhang Yong seized the tool with his hand, which was already bloodied from the work and wrapped in goat skin for protection. Zhang Wei snarled and brought the mallet down on his brother's hand. The snapping of bone was audible and the rage with which Zhang Yong body-slammed his brother was shocking, pushing him back several feet into the mortar pit, where the two rolled and struggled to rise.

Sam Wah happened to be working alongside the brothers. He ran over to break the pair apart. One of them grabbed Sam by the hair of his head, lifted his whole body and flung him across the wall, breaking out the top row of stones. While Sam lay groaning, the mighty Zhang Yong held his brother down under the thick liquid until he stopped moving. Then he got up and walked away.

Chan Yee observed the incident from two hundred yards away and by the time he got to them, there was nothing to do but clean up the mess, which he knew he should do quickly. After dragging the body out of the mortar pit, he sent one of the wheelers to notify the authorities and kept the rest of the men calm until the sheriff arrived. Zhang Yong didn't resist, and that night he was thrown into the town jail. Every man lost his supper.

While Chan Yee wrapped Sam's bruised ribs, they speculated on the events of the day.

"What do you think they'll do with him?" asked Sam.

Chan Yee raised his eyebrows. "They might hang him. But he may just disappear—I doubt we will ever see him again." It was an accurate prediction.

The construction of the wall conformed with the surface of the ridge. Occasionally difficulties arose, particularly where the crews encountered an escarpment. One mild day after a light rain, they were laying the first row of stone over a steep precipice. The crew paused to watch as Chan Yee prepared to set the heavy stone.

He and one other man rolled the huge stone to the edge where sixteen inches of space separated the limestone drop-off and the base of the wall. Chan Yee straddled the foundation, and as they lowered the stone, the soil under his right foot gave way. He fell twenty feet into a knot of scrubby brush growing out of the stone. His silent fall ended with a crash. Everyone could plainly see if he had missed the brush it would have been fatal.

Chan Yee groaned.

"Are your hurt, can you move?" shouted Sam.

"I'm okay," he said, as he began to right himself on the branch.

"Use this length of rope to tie around your waist and we will pull you up," Sam said as he uncoiled and dropped the rope to his friend.

Chan Yee slipped it around his back and tied it in front of his chest. Sam took the other end and braced it across a sapling where he and two other men held on, drawing the line carefully over the edge until the man scrambled to the top. Scratched and bruised, but not broken, Chan Yee clasped Sam's outstretched arm and grunted with relief as he was pulled to safety. He was able to stand, and of course continued the work, muttering a prayer of thanks.

After the wall was finally completed, few of the men

had saved enough money to return home. They cast about looking for work and hoping another building project would be initiated by the city's officials and businessmen.

One day Sam came running into the tent waving a placard. "Look at this," he said, pointing to the rough sheet. "They're hiring!" Someone had posted bills advertising for workers to help build a private residence. Chan Yee and his friends eagerly signed on.

The recruitment of workers for building the mansion was the first contact Chan Yee and Sam Wah had with the owner, Dr. James McNallie, a surgeon who recently moved from Memphis University Hospital, with his wife and two sons. They were a part of the exodus from Memphis after the yellow fever epidemic, and since the city had so few medical professionals—a couple of alcoholics, former army doctors practicing from a filthy clinic at the edge of town—there was a flutter of excitement among the citizens in town when he arrived. Chan Yee noted that the community threw him a dozen parties to introduce him to city society. Civic leaders also raised money for a new clinic near the center of town, at the rise of Cameron Hill, well above the flood zone.

The surgeon planned to build the new home for himself and his family, high on Mission Ridge. There were simply no existing houses fit for his family, he explained to one of his new patients.

"We need fresh air and space. The Ridge has that. And there are still plenty of laborers left in the area to build what I have in mind," Dr. McNallie postulated. Soon he had employed a sizable crew of Celestials, who had previously built the city wall, to work on his new mansion.

In the first two weeks, they dug the foundations by hand using mattocks and pickaxes and, although the ground was no longer frozen, its inconsistencies were frustrating, impeding progress from the first cornerstone.

Laid on the northeast corner of the structure, the cornerstone was engraved in an ornate Old English typeface with the name McNallie, along with the date and the architect's name—Rueben Harrison Hunt—who had only recently arrived in the community. Hunt would go on to design many important buildings that would give the city a distinctive look of its own. This home was one of his earliest works, yet a celebrated one.

The surgeon had invited the mayor to attend a small ceremony he had arranged. The head of the local freemasons also came and addressed an intimate, but distinguished, group. As the workers looked on, he formally recited the favorite institutional prayer of his organization.

"May the Great Architect of the universe enable us successfully to carry out and finish this work. May He protect the workmen from danger and accident, and long preserve the structure from decay; and may He grant us all our needed supply, the corn of nourishment, the wine of refreshment, and the oil of joy. Amen." Chan Yee was impressed with the spirit of his speech and with its blessing the work commenced enthusiastically. He was also amazed at the richness of the project. The surgeon was demanding the highest quality materials and often they had to wait months for delivery, especially for finishing touches like doorknobs and brass lamps, marble counters and mahogany handrails.

Beautiful lead glass windows were installed over the final summer's work. The men paused to gaze out at the blue sky as they put away their tools.

"The surgeon must charge very high prices to pay for these luxuries," Chan Yee said to Sam, looking around the expansive parlor with its ornately tiled fireplace.

"Yes, I hope I never need his services," Sam answered. "From the look of things, I don't think I could afford them."

CHAPTER FIVE

1995
Maddie

WHEN RUSSELL CAME home the next day, Maddie looked up from her desk and asked, "Did you bring history to life, today?" A polite, but sweeping question was one of her favorite ways to measure the mood of the man. He could be intense.

"Well, if you mean, did any of my more caffeinated students gain a new understanding of the region? Yes, I'm sure of it . . . maybe." He kissed her neck, just below the ear, and she smiled. He loved her broad smile, her fair complexion framed by soft, dark hair, brightened by astonishing seafoam eyes. A cool, delicate green, with a hint of citron—they glowed like lanterns.

Their two children were away at university and Russell knew Maddie was missing them. Nicholas had insisted on going to a different school than the one where his father taught, still a sore point for his dad. Merritt had already changed colleges twice. There was no guarantee where she would land.

The couple understood their children's need for space, and even though family was a highlight, they had active social and civic lives. Russell was a strong supporter of Cornerstone, an organization involved in historic preservation. Maddie was involved with the American Institute of Architects at state and local levels. The city's chapter was extremely active.

"The AIA wants to nominate Phillip Roberts for an award next month," Maddie announced. "Do you think he'll be ready?"

Russell remembered when they first met, feeling fortunate that she found him interesting, surrounded as she was by an edgy collection of Southern bohemians. He often wondered if he was exciting enough to be in their camp.

From Maddie's perspective, while her artist friends were wildly talented, they were also jealous of each other's success and often overly sensitive to any comment they perceived as remotely critical. She appreciated Russell's relatively calm and easygoing presence, in contrast to her group. Stoic Maddie had come from a large family, where to show any weakness would have been an invitation to torment. And yet, while these artists were sensitive to criticism, they were tolerant of each other's addictions and delusions—to a fault.

She had commissioned Phillip to paint several large canvasses for a mountain home she designed. The owner, known only as Mr. Cavanaugh from Chicago, was a mystery to her, flush with cash and amenable to the most lavish suggestions the architect made. His contemporary home was an hour from Maddie's office, on the bluff above the Tennessee River in Bridgeport, Alabama, near the Russell Cave National Monument. Russell often joked with students about the cave being named after him.

Once, Maddie had stopped to see the ancient attraction on her way back from a site visit. She thought it might inspire and inform her design. Now, inspiration didn't always come suddenly. According to Maddie, it sometimes seeped into your thoughts, appeared in your dreams, and flowed latently onto your sketchbook. At least that's how it seemed to her.

That day, as she walked toward the broad limestone entrance, she noticed the cave opened to the east, welcoming the morning sun and offering protection from winter's cold north wind. The layers of the shelf in the sunlight appeared to glow in myriad colors. A canopy of deep foliage embraced the clean lines of the cave's elongated horizontal face. Broad layers of stone stretched for almost a hundred feet from the mouth. Sunlight filtering through the trees danced on the mauve rock formations. The smooth stone ceiling above her was riddled with veins of chert, tinting it the color of terracotta. Eons of wind and water erosion had pulled the face of the cave across the woodland landscape as though it were a ribbon of clay.

Maddie had been stunned by the natural beauty. When it was finished, her creation incorporated all the elements she saw that day. Her colleagues proclaimed the façade of her design as breathtaking and they loved the layout, free flowing as the cave spring itself. The Chicagoan barely looked at the plans as he signed the hefty contract. He paid for everything in cash. A couple of years later, she heard through her connections in Birmingham that he was doing time in a federal prison for fraud and money laundering convictions. The house had been auctioned.

Phillip had benefited from their collaboration. His paintings reflected the same woodland qualities, the colors and textures of the surrounding landscape. The exterior treatment of the home used the same terra-cotta-veined limestone as the overhead ceiling of the cave. The rough cedar siding was stained in shades of pale forest green and burnt umber. Phillip used these colors in his woodland scenes, depicting streaming bars of sunlight among the trees and boulders and casting long shadows.

He was easy to work with; his addictive tendencies—apparent to Maddie over the years—were seemingly under control. He attended support group meetings at the big church on Pine Street and was maintaining a studio nearby. Several East Coast galleries represented him, and he had a growing following with some pieces in important New York collections. Selling Phillip Roberts' work for the Alabama project wasn't difficult and he began the project with enthusiasm.

The huge winter landscape of boulders and waterfalls in sepia and umber tones had worked beautifully over the fourteen-foot-wide stone fireplace that graced the end of the forty-foot great room. He had even finished by the October deadline and been paid handsomely and on time, thanks to Cavanaugh's cash dealings. Yet, three days later, Phillip went on a binge that landed him in the hospital. These were the harsh realities of working with—and loving—her friends.

"I think Phillip will come through for you," said Russell.

"I hope so. He's so talented and full of fantastic visual ideas. He needs the publicity, too."

They talked quietly over a glass of wine until she put takeout from the neighborhood Thai restaurant on the table. Russell checked his phone messages. The department had left a message about deadlines for next year's academic award approvals. Graydon Bowers' office had called to remind him of his annual exam. Russell paced back and forth across the kitchen, pausing to check his watch. Daylight was fading.

"Ugh, got a date with Dr. Gray coming up," Russell muttered.

"If it's unpleasant, why don't you change doctors?" Maddie asked. Assigning it to some misplaced loyalty, she ignored the fact that he didn't have an answer.

Four years ago, when Russell was treated for skin cancer, his brother had been the physician doing the excision and a subsequent skin graft. At the time, it felt like the right decision, because Graydon was the best in the area at what he did. Now that Russell was completely healthy, could he be associating his brother with the anxiety it caused?

It's more than that, she thought, for as likeable as Russell was, Dr. Gray Bowers was equally disliked. Even the medical society avoided him.

The Intern

Lizzer Sullivan was an intern from the university's art department and the best one Maddie's company had ever employed. She was talented and resourceful. She rarely found herself in a situation she couldn't reason through or met a client she couldn't communicate with. She often made helpful suggestions for day-to-day problems, like how to build models less expensively by using university resources and student volunteers.

Her personal life was a bit of a roller coaster ride, however, with ups and downs and hairpin turns. Her new boyfriend, Zach, was as sincere as he could be, always planning activities for them, with friends who seemed to live for energetic mountain biking and kayaking excursions.

This weekend he planned a kayaking trip around Williams' Island, one of the most beautiful places in the area. Formed by receding glaciers that deposited thousands of years of accumulated silt, it was 400-acres of heaven, according to Zach, right in the middle of the Tennessee River. Although heavenly, it still had earthly usefulness. Managed by the Tennessee River Gorge Trust, it was farmed for soybeans, used for agricultural research, and reserved for the occasional camping expedition. And the camping weekends were extremely rustic.

It seemed to her that every adventure was more challenging than the next. She wasn't sure she could continue to give up every weekend for these highly physical adventures and spend the first couple of days in the work week hobbling stiffly around the office. There *were* other things to do. Art galleries and museums, concerts and restaurants.

She loved her job at Bowers and was eager to impress its principal directors. Every day was different and a new set of challenges presented in each project they undertook. *Now isn't the best time to for a serious relationship,* she often thought. Yet, Zach was awfully cute, extremely persuasive, and *so* sincere.

Maddie

Maddie had been in the basement of the house on Mission Ridge for an hour the next morning, making space for any tile leftover from the roofing project. Her friend and associate in the firm, Joseph Kronenberg, and the intern Lizzer, had come along to help. While clearing away a corner of the south end, they noticed an irregularity. A faint seam in the wall against a massive floor beam and a red film of clay dust coating a door that had no knob—only its smooth surface giving it away—had gained their attention. They were curious, so using a crowbar to pry the door open, they sent a spray of dust through the room in the dim light of a forty-watt bulb. Stale air wafted up and they could see a stone and mortar stairway descending into darkness.

"Okay, fine," said Maddie, choking back a dry cough. "A creepy staircase under the house just adds to the charm."

Their flashlights barely penetrated the darkness as they stumbled over rubble, sliding across loose fragments like scree on a mountain slope, only to come out into a room of about fourteen-by-twenty feet.

"A storeroom," said Joseph. "Not unusual, really."

Bonnet scratched in the dirt near the southwest corner of the room. "Actually, more like a smugglers den," he continued, somewhat dramatically. He was a wellspring of architectural history.

Ten years older than Maddie, Joseph was a veteran of revitalization efforts that had taken place around the country. He had worked in Camden, New Jersey, Pittsburgh, and Baltimore, in many of the so-called legacy cities. With traditional economies built around manufacturing and populations that peaked in the twentieth century then declined to thirty to two-hundred thousand, America's small-to-midsize legacy cities could be found nationwide yet were heavily concentrated in New England and the Great Lakes region.

The city was late to start the revitalization effort, although it was rolling like a locomotive now, with foundries and warehouses across the town being transformed.

After losing his wife to cancer five years before, Joseph moved south and joined the firm. During their initial interview he told Maddie he wanted a change and to be a part of this new renaissance. "It's rewarding to see old factories repurposed and beautiful old neighborhoods revitalized."

Lizzer had been given the task of recording everything about the vintage Mission Ridge structure, from the cornerstone of the foundation to the highest chimney. She had boundless energy for artistic pursuits and, after setting up a studio light she had produced from the beat-up convertible she drove, she began snapping pictures. The extra light would make for dramatic photos, Maddie thought.

When Lizzer was finished photographing the storeroom, the trio ascended the staircase to the kitchen for Mr. T's pizza and cold beer. Lizzer's boyfriend, Zach, made the delivery, regaling them with descriptions of last night's soccer match. The stadium had been full of screaming fans—a welcome change from the decay the Southside had experienced for decades. The stadium was only a few years old but remarkably, the city's team was a regional champion, rivaled only by the Nashville Football Club.

The new stadium had also been the anchor for a dozen restaurants and breweries and for recently constructed condominiums along Fourteenth Street. Maddie knew the fast and furious growth had achieved brilliant infill, even though it was sometimes questionable as to the need for the speed of the growth. Maintaining quality was an important issue. For a certain type of resident, however, the location couldn't be better, especially for a night of exuberant entertainment. Zach, an emergency medical technician-in-training who lived in the newest building in the neighborhood, often teased Lizzer—and Maddie by proximity—about why she was so enamored with these old houses on the ridge. She didn't mind the gentle ribbing, especially when it came, as it frequently did, with a side of pizza.

Maddie finished her slice and refilled her water bottle.

"I think I left my gloves downstairs, I'll be right back," she said. She constantly misplaced them even though they were her favorite pair. Thin, well-fitting work gloves of goatskin leather were hard to find and harder to keep.

Down the stairs she charged, careful to avoid the loose masonry. As she walked across the open space, toward the newly discovered basement room, she felt a wave of cold air sweep over her. She spotted her gloves lying just outside the door and bent down to pick them up. As she stood up, she thought she saw a movement in the doorway, barely illuminated by soft light from the vents at the end of the room. When she looked directly through the door, she stared hard, trying to focus on what must surely be a hallucination. It seemed to be the figure of a man, slowly turning around to face her. The man eyed her coldly and then moved away and disappeared, as though in a dream. When she went to the door, there was nothing there. Drawing her breath in sharply, she began to shiver as she made for the stairway. She was up the stairs and running into the kitchen, almost panting as she gathered up her things.

"Lizzer, I . . . I forgot I have an appointment. I'll meet you back at the office," she said abruptly, tearing out of the kitchen and down the veranda. The girl just stared.

What could Maddie possibly say? Her friends would think she was crazy if she told what she *thought* she saw,

THE INNER WALL | 37

and maybe she was. She tried to shake it off. Needing time to think, she drove to the City Planning Center to review a request on a project she was interested in bidding on. The radio streamed an old Santana song as the summer heat vibrated from the dashboard. She chatted with a few colleagues on the way in, picked up the materials and by the time she left the building and had gotten across town the illusion seemed so unlikely, that she mentally dismissed it from her mind and almost from her memory.

Gray

As Russell drove toward the town center, down the steep grade of second street, past luxury condominiums and specialty shops, he tried to remember a time when he and Gray had been close and came up with nothing. His only sibling had been a shadow moving at the edge of his world.

Now he hurried into his brother's medical office, a few minutes late. It wasn't until the nurse called him, ten minutes later, that he realized the office had been redecorated again—the third time in two years. Russell sat in the exam room for another forty-five minutes, his blood pressure on the rise. When Gray appeared, his bleached and toothy smile shined bright as he looked down on his brother, a glint in his eyes.

On the surface, Gray was a faded version of his younger sibling. At sixty-two, he appeared to control his world. His privileged upbringing had set him on the road to distinction, but somehow, he was missing the empathetic response to his fellow man that his parents and brother so strongly possessed. In fact, he seemed to resent his mother's kindness and his father's philanthropy.

"Russ," Gray said. He delivered every word in a pinched nasal tone. "It's been such a busy morning. Sorry for the delay, but I know you educators have plenty of time on your hands. How's Maddie?"

"Fine. She's busy with the firm," Russell responded obligingly. "And renovating the house."

His brother didn't reply, studying him with what seemed to be contempt. After a cursory exam and a few questions, the doctor entered a few comments into the computer, then scribbled an order onto a yellow form, sending the patient to the lab. Before he left the room, he turned back to Russell.

"Say, I can take that dump off your hands, if you'd like to flip it. Real estate fever has totally gripped the practice. Everyone's investing."

"It's not a dump, Gray." Russell lowered his voice, reminding himself to keep an even tone despite all desires to the contrary. "I'd never sell it, in fact."

"You should give it some thought," Gray said. Then the doctor was gone.

Russell frowned, buttoned his shirt, picked up the yellow form and went out. As glitzy as the waiting room had been, the long fluorescent-lit hallway was grim.

CHAPTER SIX

1889
Chan Yee

CHAN YEE NOTICED that Dr. McNallie's practice grew over time. His wealth increased and his ego along with it. In the early days, the surgeon's work elevated and distinguished him. Yet, it was still a small community and his need for more power, wealth and recognition seemed to become an obsession. It had taken several years to build the mansion and it was, undoubtedly, the most glamorous house in the area. Now to pay off the workers and announce its completion.

When Sam signed the lease agreement for the two-room building down in the hollow on River Street, Chan Yee was there to help celebrate and set up the stockroom. Boxes of dried beans and other staples had already begun to be delivered. His own lease on the laundry had recently been finalized. He was excited, the mansion was finally finished. He felt just as elated as he had been when the wall was finished, but this time Chan Yee had a plan.

He and Sam headed up the ridge to pick up their final pay. Now that the mansion was complete, a photographer from the newspaper was coming up to get a photograph of the house, its owner and even the work crew. He watched as the flashy little man moved things around to set up for the photograph and was reminded of an actor he had seen in a traveling Chinese theatre, a time long ago.

"Wah . . . Yee," their names were called out, from under a white tent at the job site. "Here's your pay. Now go and stand over there with the others so Cedric can get his picture and get out of our way." Somehow, gathering for a photographic record of the work they had accomplished seemed like a proper end to the project. When he was finished with the group, the bustling photographer hurried up the hill to where the family had finally gathered in front of the house to have their portrait made. With money in their pockets, the workmen scurried away to eagerly pursue their own plans. It was an optimistic beginning for their budding enterprises.

The next day, Chan Yee opened the door of the laundry to an insistent knock. There was Sam, eager to see the new establishment.

"Come in," he said, opening the door wider. Inside, a barefoot youth of about twelve stirred a vat of clothing, the scent of soap heavy in the steamy air. Across the room a young woman was engrossed in her sewing. She had a thin red ribbon woven into her hair and held at least a dozen pins between her lips. She snatched the pins away from her mouth and glanced up as the stranger entered.

"Sam, this is Ida. She is our seamstress." Chan Yee couldn't help but notice Sam's eyes widen as he took in the sight. Ida smiled and said hello. Chan Yee heard the whistle of the tea kettle and set out three cups. He filled them with his best oolong. It was time to celebrate.

"How is the store coming, Sam?" Chan Yee wanted to know. "Will we be able find everything we need there?"

"I hope you will. It would be nice to have a woman's view on the stock, just in case I have overlooked something." He glanced at Ida as she took a sip of her tea. "Maybe you could stop by?" Ida smiled again.

Sam Wah

One afternoon in midwinter, the surgeon stopped for tobacco at a small shop on West Ninth Street near the river docks, not one he usually frequented. In fact, he knew his wife would be horrified if she saw him there. She wouldn't see him, however, and neither would she hear about it, for there were no other customers like him. A potbelly stove in the corner warmed the small store where a couple of Chinese men talked quietly while they played a game that was unfamiliar to Dr. McNallie. He chose a tin of tobacco, paid for it, and asked to speak to the owner, although he knew he was already speaking to him. He recognized Sam Wah from the construction crew that built his house.

Wah was hard working and seemed to have many connections. Dr. McNallie believed the Chinese had a network to acquire certain drugs with incredible powers. And these powers were just what he needed. Using their tinctures in his compounds, he would be able to increase the number of patients who would pay handsomely for them. A pharmacist in Georgia was already using them in a variety of products, but Dr. McNallie had a suspicion it would not last, and he'd need an ample supply for the future.

"Listen, Wah," he spoke in a low tone. "I need you to order a shipment of laudanum."

"I don't have laudanum."

"But you know how to get it. The meager supply I can acquire barely meets the needs of the practice," the doctor whined. He had a business idea he wanted to try and was sure these Celestials had a direct, cheap, and undocumented supply. But Sam lowered his eyes and said no more. The surgeon stormed out.

After the surgeon's visit, Sam closed the store early and went to see Ida at the laundry. The bell jangled as he stepped inside and saw her working at a long table, standing while she pinned a piece of silk lining to a handsome tweed fabric. She looked up and gave him a beautiful smile.

"Hi Sam!"

"Hello, Ida. I was wondering if I could make supper for you. We have an extra basket of fresh peaches at the store."

"Oh, I would like that. Let me just finish what I'm doing here."

"What are you working so hard on?" he asked.

"A new suit for the mayor," she said rather proudly. She had taken the measurements of the city's new mayor and had worked from one of his old suits to redesign a new one. She had ordered quality fabrics and notions, and although it took time, it was more exciting than the usual piece mending she did for the laundry.

"Sam, you've torn the pocket of your jacket," she said, gesturing to the tear, as he stood near her at the table. "Let me sew that up for you."

After supper and a dish of peach cobbler, they talked about their families. Sam grew still and reflective.

"I grew up along the coast and my father fished. We were fortunate to have food when so many others didn't, but when the boat was destroyed in a storm, I had to find work and that brought me to this place."

"I'm glad you found your way here," she said softly.

That evening when he walked her home, he left the jacket with her at the door. As she gathered it up, she smelled his own slightly spicy scent, mingled with fresh peaches. The next day the repair was flawless and, when he tried to pay her, she refused.

Sam did not wait long. A week later, on a buoyant Sunday afternoon, they walked along a woodland trail near the river pausing beside a huge limestone boulder.

"I have something for you," Sam said as he pulled a small paper wrapper from his pocket. Opening it, he put the delicate bracelet of pearls around her wrist and kissed her hand.

"Ida, will you marry me?" he asked directly.

She held his face in her hands and said, "I was afraid you weren't going to ask."

Ida was beautiful, particularly her bright smile. When he was with her, Sam felt as though he was on a mountaintop, breathing clear, clean air. His admiration for her grew until he thought his heart would burst. With her by his side, he could justify the harsh years of labor. She understood both the hardship and the isolation from his homeland. She was his reward and theirs was an impetuous love. Sensual and kind, but in plain sight, there for all to see.

The question of race was like a cloud that would loom overhead and then glide away, leaving them in the sunlight again. He came to church with her, ignoring the frowns of the righteous, until one Sunday they began to accept him.

"I'm happy to see you here today, Mr. Wah," said

Mary Lou Adams, with her baby on her arm and a toddler peeking from the folds of her skirt. "The other night when Daniel was sick, my husband was so glad your store was just around the corner."

Blue Goose Hollow had never had a market before. The tiny enclave was home to nearly eighty laborers and their families.

For the locals, Sam's store had teething powders for their infants, baking soda for their bread, lye soap and boot polish. It had more variety than they had ever known, and the merchandise was available at fair prices. More importantly, the door was never closed to them. For the Chinese, the store stocked good, quality Siamese rice and aromatic camphor—a perfume, food, and a cure for everything from cataracts to evil vapors of the heart. Gradually, at least among their customers, Sam and Ida's romance was becoming more acceptable, if only because he was providing a service they needed.

Getting someone to marry the couple proved to be the obstacle that troubled them most. They wanted—*needed*— to be together. They shared with each other the favorite traditions of their cultures, their folklore. They took comfort together in a religion that originally would have belonged to neither of them. Yet, every time they approached the sixty-seven-year-old minister about their ceremony, he just shook his head and said, "No, it wouldn't be right." In fact, he seemed to enjoy telling them no.

Finally, a young and idealistic preacher visiting family in the area was invited to speak at the New Monumental Church. When he met Sam and Ida, he thought they were either crazy, or they must truly represent the future. He rallied behind the futuristic theory and performed a quiet service, with only Sam's former coworkers, Chan Yee, Chan Ock and Mrs. Adams in attendance as witnesses. Ida wore a light blue dress and borrowed gloves. Mrs. Adams pinned a white peony to her small, feather-gray hat.

Their friends were glad to see them so happy and were fascinated by the preacher. During the ceremony, the man spoke eloquently of prophets who would usher in an age of acceptance and freedom none had experienced before.

"They will seal the vow with the sacrifice of blood," he attested. "The world to come is made for people of faith, hope and love. And the greatest of these is love."

When he pronounced them man and wife, Sam's eyes glistened, and his wide smile revealed the dimple in his chin. He lifted Ida into the air and kissed her.

Ida

That night after the ceremony, Ida moved into Sam's house near the docks, bringing her belongings—her aunt's clock, a small case of clothing, a box of dishes and two baskets of sewing projects she was working on for people in the community. She had never known her mother. She had grown up instead with her aunt and three cousins. It was her aunt who taught her to sew.

The eldest of the cousins was Carver, who everyone hoped would become a minister. But he had worked in his youth for Oakland where his mother was the head housekeeper. It was the only farm in the area large enough to breed and produce fine carriage horses. Carver became an expert horse trainer even as the world was soon to be dazzled by the advent of the automobile. The other cousins both married ministers and moved to Atlanta.

Ida's aunt had died two years earlier and she had begun to feel rather alone when Chan Yee asked her to do some alterations for his laundry business. She admired the way the Celestials took control of their lives through their small enterprises.

When she met Sam Wah, she would never have imagined she would be so lucky to find real love with someone she truly admired. Someone smart who worked hard, was fair and kind. They enjoyed their modest life together and satisfied each other completely.

"You would never know we didn't come from the same tribe," she said with a grin one night. The firelight made her face glow.

"We do. The secret tribe," he said softly. He walked over and began to unbutton her dress. "Let me help you rest from your labor," he said as he took the needle from her grip, secured it in the woolen fabric of the waist coat she was working on and placed it back into the basket.

As his hand invaded her dress from the nape, down her back, he spoke to her softly of her beauty and his gratitude that she was his to love. He tugged at the sleeves and pulled the dress away, then lifting her, he carried her to the bed. His lips found her breasts, his hands moved between her legs. They spent the best part of the night gently rolling, undulating in the bedclothes until an exhausted stillness and contented sleep took them.

Chan Yee

A few weeks after their wedding, Chan Yee observed Sam and Ida sitting on a row near the back of the New Monumental Church. He sat down nearby while members greeted each other warmly. They laughed and talked until the preacher entered the pulpit and took up his Bible. He always opened with an urgency, a pent-up energy, as though his thoughts had been building all week. Like a cloud that was twisting and tightening, about to break forth in a new direction, he would begin his sermon with explosive passion.

The little flock was largely made up of formerly enslaved people who did not want to return to the farm to work as sharecroppers. Most of them lived in shanties by the river, many of them shoveling coal on the steamboats that hissed their way from Natchez to Kingston. Some of them, like old Jem Johnson and Moses Adams, had even worked on the General Jackson, docked in Nashville on the Cumberland River. Their calloused hands and crooked fingers had endured years of struggle. Some had scarred arms and faces from boiler explosions. The boats were now gradually being pushed aside as the preferred method of moving goods and people by the new extensions of the railway system, unbound as they were to any body of water.

There were a few craftsmen in the congregation, a smithy or two, and others who worked as draymen, making deliveries to the northernmost tip of the county. Still others hired out for day work and farm labor during cotton and tobacco harvests. When all else failed to produce income, the local hog farmer offered the lowest wages to those who were willing.

The congregation's energy was a living force, and on Sunday it swelled beyond the tiny sanctuary, with shouting and singing spilling out into the community.

Reverend Thirkill entered and climbed the pulpit to begin reading from the scriptures. Few among the congregation could read, so he did not ask them to follow along.

"Lord God," he began, pleading with the heavens, "bless this reading of your word."

The Fall of Jericho—Joshua 5: 13-15

Now when Joshua was near Jericho, he looked up and saw a man standing in front of him with a drawn sword in his hand. Joshua went up to him and asked, "Are you for us or for our enemies?"

"Neither," he replied, "but as commander of the army of the Lord I have now come." Then Joshua fell facedown to the ground in reverence, and asked him, "What message does my Lord have for his servant?"

The commander of the Lord's army replied, "Take off your sandals, for the place where you are stand-ing is holy."

At this, Reverend Thirkill slammed his large hand onto the white-washed podium, its hollow chest booming like thunder. A few small boys on the second row jumped and a chorus of amens circulated in the Sunday morning congregation of about forty-five. Light streamed in through rose-colored windows. The Reverend's large frame filled the pulpit, the contrast of his dark suit against the white walls and the dark string tie against his starched white shirt created a visual vibration for the faithful.

"They were standing on *holy* ground," the Reverend reiterated. "The children of Israel had crossed the Jordan River going into the promised land," he said, waving as if to indicate the great distance.

"Moses had died over there in Moab, after he saw the land from the mountaintop. He could not lead them in, but he had ordained Joshua to lead them in," the reverend explained. "I wonder, was Joshua afraid? Did he understand what he was supposed to do? So much responsibility, so much trouble. The Israelites had been through so much, and now, when they finally crossed the river to go into the land, they come up against *a wall*. How would they get in?" Reverend Thirkill paused for emphasis. "We sometimes find ourselves on the outside—looking in!" Again, his hand slammed against the podium. "Well brothers and sisters, when you find yourself on the outside, *what do you do?*"

"We pray, Lord, pray," called the congregants. "Amen."

"Here they were, camped on the plain of Jericho outside the city wall and ready to fight, but just like He had promised, the Lord would do *amazing* things." The reverend's voice rose in a jubilant cry. He was beginning to perspire. "God's children were on the *outside*. God had promised them the land—a land flowing with milk and honey— but here they were on the *outside*. Sometimes, we are, too—on the outside looking in."

He raised his Bible high over his head.

"The Lord told Joshua to take the fighting men and march around the city one time, every day for six days. On the first day, they marched. On the second day, they marched. On the third day, they marched. And onward, to the sixth day. What was Joshua thinking? Well, we know he was *faithful*. The Holy Scriptures tell us he was *obedient*.

"On the seventh day, the Lord said to send the seven priests blowing their rams' horns and march around the city *seven* times," he shouted. "And Joshua said, 'be quiet until I tell you to shout.' Did Joshua understand? No. But he believed.

"Just like the Lord sometimes sends us out to do what

we don't understand. We must pay attention, brothers and sisters. We must keep our faith. We must build each other up. Not only that—we must be willing to *cross* the river, ready to *shout* until the wall falls down.

"Listen to the poetry," he said. "Hear the word."

Joshua 6:15-20

> *On the seventh day they got up at daybreak and marched around the city in the same manner, except on that day they circled the city seven times. The seventh time around, when the priests sounded the trumpet blast, Joshua commanded the people, "Shout, for the Lord has given you the city!"*

"Joshua *was* paying attention, brothers and sisters. The Lord would give him the city—*amen!*" An eruption of 'bless him, Lord' and 'amen' rumbled through the little sanctuary as the Reverend paused to take out his handkerchief and mop his forehead. He picked up the book again and shouted, "Hear the word!"

> *When the trumpets sounded, the army shouted, and at the sound of the trumpet, when the men gave a loud shout, the wall collapsed; so, everyone charged straight in, and they took the city.*

"Be ready children, because when God calls, we will cross the river. We will shout out. The wall is sure to fall. And we will enter the promised city, where there is opportunity for everyone—Hallelujah!"

Songs rose from the congregation like rolling waves, lasting well into the midday when they finally fanned out into the churchyard toward tables spread with every homemade comestible, there under the trees. Later there would be a baptism at the river's edge.

Sam and Ida joined Chan Yee where he stood under a huge oak tree, enjoying the breeze and a piece of fried chicken.

"Have you made arrangements to fetch your bride?" asked Ida after a sip of iced tea. "We're excited to meet her, aren't we, Sam?"

Chan Yee smiled broadly. "Soon," he said. "Soon."

Ida

That winter, Ida became ill. She was seized by severe cramps in her side and began vomiting. She did not improve, and as her fever climbed higher, Sam hitched his mule to the wagon and took her from their store to the Cameron Hill clinic. The surgeon could help, but would he?

No doubt they would normally have been turned away, but the surgeon saw them coming. An opportunity walking in his door. The clinic was still unpainted and waiting for finishing trim at the windows and eaves. The solitary nurse and her aide were instructed by the surgeon to help Ida undress and lie under a sheet on the examining table. The skin of her abdomen was stretched and bloated, her eyes wide with fear, her beautiful face ashen.

After examining Ida, Dr. McNallie turned to Sam.

"Your wife has acute appendicitis. Have you heard of it?" He didn't bother to wait for a response. "She will die without surgery. I can't be sure she won't die anyway. But we have anesthesia and I know the procedure." Surgical treatment was all the rage, in fact, ever since Harvard professor and Massachusetts physician Reginald Fitz had documented and named the condition. Remarkably, the first successful surgery had been performed in London in 1735 at St. George's Hospital.

The surgeon had assisted with several appendectomies in his early career at the hospital in Memphis and he had been among the observers in the surgical theater at Roosevelt Hospital in New York City.

After explaining the procedure to his head nurse and her assistant, he set about to transform one of the examining rooms into a surgical stage. He was a follower of the British physician Joseph Lister who was a pioneer of antiseptic surgery. Applying Louis Pasteur's advances in microbiology, Lister had introduced carbolic acid to sterilize surgical instruments and clean wounds. It was the surgeon's belief in the disinfectant and a generous supply he had procured that helped make his surgery room a success.

While his nurse sprayed the equipment and arranged the lamplights near the patient, he reviewed his notebook on the procedure and then prepared the abdomen for the incision.

The nurse covered the patient's mouth and nose with a square of white coarsely woven cotton and began allowing light drops of ether onto the square so that she ceased her moaning. Her body was draped in bleached cotton sheets. The tray positioned at the surgeon's side was covered with his instruments of choice and a bowl to receive the pathetic organ if it could be retrieved without bursting.

Sam was shooed into the outer reception room, where he stayed alone, staring at gray walls and listening to the ominous rhythm of the wall clock. He drifted into a restless sleep in which he dreamed he was once again building the wall, and for every stone he laid there were three more rows to go. He awoke fearful and far from rested. He was relieved when the surgeon came in to tell him the procedure had been a success.

"You can take her home in the morning, but it will be several days before she should move around, longer before she can lift anything. If the incision becomes red or swollen and her fever returns, bring her back. He gave Sam some medicine for Ida to use in the days to come. He wrote down a date and time for a follow-up appointment on a small piece of paper and handed it to Sam.

"So, how do you expect to pay?" the surgeon asked, his face contorting for emphasis. "I must increase my supply of laudanum and I know it is available." Sam was calm, and except for the tiny beads of perspiration on his forehead near the hairline, unmoved. He was a study in restraint.

"I can pay. It may take some time to find a supply, but I will pay," said Sam.

"Just find it and quickly," he snapped, sure that Sam had the ability to purchase from some unknown source. "You owe me."

"I will," he said.

The fact that it was to come from a source Sam really did not have, was not to stop him from agreeing to get it. He would find a supplier. So, in this way the Wahs became subjugated to the surgeon and soon this yoke would become heavier than either of them could have imagined.

When Ida did not come to work the following morning, Chan Yee stopped by to see if anything was wrong. Sam explained what had happened and shared his frustration with his friend. The problem was clear to Chan Yee and he suggested they ask Chan Ock and the others for help.

In fact, Chan Ock knew a traveling merchant who brought goods from San Francisco across country by train and then up the Ohio River to the Tennessee. But the opium was for smoking. So, he wrote to a cousin in New Orleans, where shipments of quality morphine and laudanum came in regularly. Arrangements were made, and the first case was paid for with the money Sam and Ida usually used to reorder stock for the store, plus some of their meager savings. Chan Yee advanced wages to Ida through the end of the month.

Ida's surgery had been a success. She was recuperating, her color had returned, and the fever was gone. Now, her shock at the price of her medical miracle had taken over.

"He can't force us to do this!"

"We'll be done with it soon, Ida," Sam reassured. He stood on a stepstool filling the high shelf with cans of baking powder, his trim athletic frame, backlit by the shop window. "Now that he has a way to get the laudanum directly from Chan Ock's cousin, he won't need us anymore."

The stitches were removed without incident and Ida's routine went back to normal. She spent more time helping Sam at the store, since business was good. The Blue Goose Hollow neighborhood was packed with people, and they began to think it might be possible to expand the store into the empty storage space next door. She could discuss the possibilities for hours.

They dreamed of adding a section of smoked meats and flour from a miller up the river, in addition to the local cornmeal. A friend was making jams and jellies they would begin selling at the end of the summer season and then she would make candies for Christmas. If they kept the prices down, the people could afford an occasional luxury. Despite the surgeon and his subterfuge, their hopes and plans flourished.

"There's a farm below Oakland where we can buy

sorghum syrup and Mary Granger is making brown butter caramels and pralines next month," said Sam, with more than a little excitement. "It's been impossible to get cane sugar, even if you wanted it." He finished unloading twenty pounds of sweet potatoes into a large willow basket Ida had placed at the end of the counter. He turned toward the store's one window and saw more people than he had seen in months out on a Saturday afternoon.

The bell jangled on the door and Chan Yee came in to pick up boot polish.

"How have you been," he asked. "Ida, can you spare a few days next week to help me catch up with my orders?"

She smiled. "Surely. I have to keep my hand in, in case the grocery business fails."

Ida had almost forgotten the tension created by the surgeon's tonic enterprise until there were rumors of an expected shortage of laudanum that spring. Indeed, shipments came later and later throughout the months of May and June. It was said that production had become slow and haphazard.

A few of the surgeon's patients had complained about the consistency of the tonic and others had read negative magazine articles about long-term use of the opiate. A Nashville newspaper had even reported a death related to the drug.

Every time she thought they were through dealing with the surgeon he somehow imposed himself on Sam with some wild request—as though Sam was his personal servant.

CHAPTER SEVEN

1995
Zee

ZEE LUNSFORD WAS only days past finishing the final chapter of her new book on the influence of grandparents. The stream of her clients had thinned in the last year, so when Maddie called to invite her to lunch, she gladly accepted the offer.

With Maddie's distinct preference for ethnic foods, naturally, she suggested they have lunch at Taqueria Jalisco on Rossville Avenue. Zee might have chosen a different restaurant—although the menu was limited—she knew the chicken was fresh, the rice was fluffy, and the floors were clean.

So the next day they were seated near a sunny window on the street side of the tiny establishment. Two other tables were busy with lunch customers. Maddie ordered the house burrito and Zee had the Guatemalan interpretation of gazpacho.

"Have you seen how good the new roof looks?" Maddie asked. "You should come down the street and get a closer look."

"I will," she said as she produced a calendar from her small handbag and arranged the date then and there. Zee left no detail hanging in the air.

The two friends made small talk—the hotel project, Vivienne's prep school— before Maddie finally raised the subject she had been brooding over. Hearing about the Bowers' sibling relationship, Zee's dark eyes grew rounder. Maddie knew her friend relished a family struggle.

"I'm afraid I don't know Dr. Bowers very well," said Zee. "But I do have an older brother, and they *can* be overbearing."

"Are you still in the South Broad office, Zee?"

"No, a new practice is occupying that space now—all drum circles and experimental therapies, you know," she offered with a wrinkle of her nose. "Now I use the morning room in my own home, where there is plenty of space."

"I don't know much about their early relationship, but Russell and Gray have never really been close," Maddie remarked. "When he was married, he and his wife were awfully unpleasant to be around because either they argued, or he was sullen and withdrawn. We've never been able to make a connection. I've often wondered if something traumatic happened to him."

"So many events in one's childhood are important, but so layered over, often quite forgotten. From molestation to bullying, time has a way of submerging unpleasant memories if the adverse episodes end. Yet, submerged memories have a way of bubbling up.

"Many years ago, I counseled a man who was having panic attacks when he made presentations for his job, even though he had never experienced a problem with it before. His body was wracked by a blast of heat followed by dizziness and nausea, then a cold sweat. These high-level corporate presentations were a huge part of his work. But now, they were making him sick and his inability to complete them was affecting his job," said Zee.

"We slowly and carefully peeled back the layers of his adolescence, like peeling an artichoke, uncovering the harsh retribution of an alcoholic father who constantly berated his schoolwork and frequently beat him. After his parents' divorce, the scenes of violent humiliation were pushed into the cracks of his unconscious mind."

"What happened?"

"With substantial emotional effort, he began facing these memories. It took time. "You know, even the charmed life can be hard. One minute you're in control, on top—the next minute, not so. I thought aging would be somehow more profound," she said. "A finishing touch, a crowning jewel, icing on the cake? It isn't.

"I've been many selves. I know how things fit together and can see the epic picture, but my own private humor is the characteristic of these collective years that I find most pleasurable. Irony is evident all around."

Maddie

After lunch, Maddie drove over to the Wheelhouse, where she expected to meet Joseph, along with the project manager and construction supervisors. Instead, she pulled into a parking lot bathed in the flashing blue light of a police car. She grabbed her cell phone and her hard hat and walked over to the knot of men standing outside the Wheelhouse's main entrance.

"What's going on?" Maddie asked the group. She could see Joseph in the side lot, examining a palette of windows that had been pulled across the gravel. Several of them were shattered. The Wheelhouse's exterior wall had been spray-painted, the primitive black lines depicting figures that looked like holocaust victims. Angry gun-wielding images exploded down the exterior wall. A slow train rolled along the tracks behind the building. It too, was adorned with graffiti. In contrast—soft, colorful, exuberant.

"You're Mrs. Bowers, I'm guessing?" asked an older officer.

Maddie nodded.

"Vandalism,' the officer continued. "Your associate, Mr. Kronenberg, says these windows were delivered late yesterday, after almost everyone had gone home. I'll need to see the delivery ticket, ask the truck driver if he saw anything."

After forty-five minutes of more questions, the officer left to file his report.

"We'll have the building watched for the next few nights," he told Maddie and Joseph before climbing into his patrol car. "You should really get some cameras installed."

After the commotion, the meeting with the site supervisors dragged on. It was difficult to concentrate and finally Maddie rescheduled it for the next day. She felt heavy with worry as she got into her SUV, popped the clutch, and headed into traffic on West Main.

The outside brick of the Turnbull Building, where the office was, felt like the wall of an oven at this point in the afternoon, and it would only get worse over the next few hours. The stifling humidity made it difficult to breathe, and Maddie's hair frizzed away from her scalp in protest. The blue hydrangeas on the shadier side of the building entrance were limp and drooping. There it was, buyer's remorse. It swelled in the pit of her stomach, adding to the sense of suffocation from the heat.

Once inside, Maddie climbed up the open steel staircase, its modern design showcased against the early nineteenth century exposed brick wall. A gigantic oil painting by Marvella Bukari hung above the second-floor mezzanine—a girl with her hair in braids, wearing boots and a red polka-dot dress, flying over a green meadow. Fourteen-foot windows made the space feel like a cathedral. The combination of the spare contemporary interior design and the idiosyncratic detail of the industrial space was poetry to Maddie. The cooler, lighter air revived her.

Once in the office, Lizzer handed her a contact sheet and the disc bearing her photos from the Mission Ridge house. Maddie noted how pleased she seemed.

"You're going to love these," she said, upbeat as always. "Oh, Mr. Clark is in the small conference room for you."

John Harrison Clark was an astute real estate agent, but he was lucky, too. Always in the right place at the most fortunate time, he rode the trends of urban redevelopment like a rodeo star. His broad shoulders and square jaw added to the persona. He attended every charrette and watched the decisions of the planning commission with rapt attention. He had also married into old money and was privy to early insider information. A handy detail.

"Some papers for you to sign, Maddie," he said. He was only one of many developers and agents she worked with, but he may have been her favorite. Calm, forthright and drawn to projects that always turned out to be profitable, she trusted his instincts.

"How's the house coming along?" he asked as she looked over the paperwork. "You had some upgrades planned, didn't you?"

"A new roof. That'll be the biggest expense this year. Although, we're working on the downstairs kitchen and bathrooms." She looked up from the papers. "Did you know there's a room under the basement?"

"Is it a finished space?" he asked with a grin. "If I'd known that I might have tried to claim the extra square footage.

"By the way, what's all this interest from your brother-in-law? He was pretty angry with me when he found out we'd put the house back on the market without letting him know." John rarely involved himself with residential sales, but the entire Mission Ridge neighborhood was being recreated and he'd told Maddie he couldn't pass up such a significant project. "I probably should have let him know before I called you. I just hate talking to him."

Maddie laughed and slid the papers back across the table. "You're not the only one! Life is too short!"

When John left, Maddie returned to her office, where Lizzer had laid out the workprint photos of the house from rooftop to basement. She noticed two dark images of the basement stairs, oddly lit from the room below so that it gave the edge of the stairs the appearance of jagged teeth. The room beyond the spotlight was lamp black. Lizzer was a good photographer, but Maddie wondered if she was playing with this, just a bit? Then she remembered the figure in the basement.

Trying to overcome a sensation of panic, she left the office feeling anxious and stopped by the Flying Kite for a drink. She wanted to review the events of the past few days and think about the things that had to be done during the week ahead.

The little bar was sleek and new. Her friends all loved it,

and it was a place they felt comfortable. The glass walls on the southwest side took in the neighborhood. As the sun sank lower into the wooded horizon, broken only by café signs, school buildings, and church steeples, she looked up to see Zach come in. He almost walked past.

"Hello, Zach," called Maddie.

"Hey, I didn't see you. Lizzer is supposed to be meeting me here."

"Oh, sorry. She's running an errand for me up on the mountain," she said with a guilty look. "Maybe it won't make her too late. Why don't you join me?

"This is the one place I don't mind enjoying a drink alone—but then you're always pretty sure your mother wouldn't like it," Maddie said.

"Since when did you worry about what your mother thought?"

"As long as she was alive, and then some."

He chuckled as he sank into the chair, plopping a thick blue folder down on the gray laminate of the table.

"What's this?" She pointed to the folder.

"Well, you won't believe it, but I've completed my essay on the origin of opiates for the last quarter of the EMT program."

"Congratulations," said Maddie. She had heard some of his war stories.

"You know, you're lucky. One hundred years ago, society didn't think it was proper for women to come to bars and drink, so they stayed home and used opiates instead, to relieve the stress and strain," he laughed, although he didn't really think it was funny. He had to deal with the legacy of drug use every day.

"Tell me about your paper."

"You seriously want to hear about it?"

"Sure."

Zach pulled out a timeline and said, "Here goes. As early as 3400 BC, the history of the opium poppy was recorded in lower Mesopotamia. The Sumerians called it the 'joy plant' and they passed the plant with its euphoric effects on to the Assyrians. From there it was traded to the Babylonians, who in turn, enlightened the Egyptians. Alexander the Great introduced it throughout Persia and India in 330 BC. By 460 BC Hippocrates acknowledged its usefulness in treating internal diseases."

"I always thought it came from China," interjected Maddie.

"Actually, it wasn't until AD 400 that it was brought to China by Arab traders. The Portuguese modeled the smoking of opium as they sailed the East China Sea in 1500—although to the Chinese it was a barbaric and subversive habit.

"During the height of the Reformation, opium was re-introduced in European medical literature by Paracelsus as laudanum. The black pills were made of opium, citrus juice and quintessence of gold, and were prescribed as painkillers.

"Dutch traders sent shipments of Indian opium to China for use in tobacco pipes, although Chinese Emperor Yung Cheng issued an edict in 1729, prohibiting the smoking of opium and its domestic sale except under license for use as medicine. It was a good policy, that was tested continually and eventually failed. Although it was repeatedly banned in the huge China market, opium was constantly brought in by American and British smugglers.

"In the early 1600s ships chartered by Elizabeth the first were instructed to "purchase the finest Indian opium" and transport it back to England. By 1793, the British East India Company had established a monopoly on the opium trade in India where the business grew more lucrative with each passing year."

"That was quite a big business."

"Yes, it was and it grew bigger and more powerful. John Jacob Astor of New York City got in on the action when his American Fur Company bought ten tons of Turkish opium, shipping the contraband to Canton. Astor later left the China opium trade and sold chiefly to England.

"The First Opium War began on March 18, 1839, when British ships attacked in response to China's suppression of the opium trade. The Chinese were defeated, and Hong Kong was ceded to the British. The Second Opium War in 1856 was once again lost by China and after the country was forced to pay an indemnity, the importation of opium was legalized."

"What happened in the States?" said Maddie.

"Ironically, in San Francisco, smoking opium was banned by officials and confined to Chinatown. In the late 1890s, publisher William Randolph Hearst ran lurid stories in his nationally distributed tabloids of white women seduced by Chinese men. Opium was the lure."

"You say turn-of-the-century society women used opium in the privacy of their homes, but now you see mostly meth addiction here in the South," said Maddie.

"It's cheaper and some states prioritize opiate addiction over methamphetamine addiction, making intensive treatment for uninsured meth users hard to come by," Zach responded. Just then Lizzer walked in.

"Hey, what's going on? Social time without me?"

"More like a history lesson," said Maddie, finishing her drink. "Congrats on completing your coursework, Zach." She picked up her satchel, keys and sunglasses and headed out to meet Russell with a growing respect for Lizzer's new boyfriend.

CHAPTER EIGHT

1890
Margaret

MARGARET MONTAIGNE WAITED for the driver to open the door of the carriage at the surgeon's office. She stepped lightly onto the gravel path in front of the gray clapboard building. Walking past a dried-up flowerbed, she went inside and twenty minutes later reemerged holding a brown paper wrapper. She got back into the carriage.

Margaret had been a patient of the surgeon since her second miscarriage. He had a brilliant elixir for her pain, and it seemed to soothe her emotional distress too. Elaborate displays of emotion had been the expression of choice for her mother who had wanted to be a stage actress, but married a steel executive from Pennsylvania instead. Her father, on the other hand showed no emotion whatsoever. Calculating and cynical, he could be a mean drunk. When sober, he barely noticed his daughter at all. They were self-absorbed parents at best.

The boredom of being a daughter in a home where one had so little value and no voice in her future was suffocating, but not unusual. Margaret was married off to the first man who came to call. One who wanted a place for himself in society. So in the spring, she and Henry B. Montaigne were married and although she found he didn't actually listen to her—he made all the decisions about where they would live and who they would socialize with—she was hopeful that when her children were born, she would have something meaningful in her life. Henry's expectations had to do with career advancement.

"I'm next in line," he told his favorite bartender. "Soon I'll be vice president at the bank." His wife's prominent family had given him some notoriety. He kept up with the events of the day, stopping at the tavern almost every night to discuss politics and local scandal, often arriving home after dinner had been cleared away. At first Margaret complained, but then she became used to this. Thinking his wife was a bit hysterical, he was both bored and distracted, and often distracted by other women. While Henry was ambitious, he was not terribly smart.

It hadn't always been this way, she occasionally reflected. In the early years of their marriage, he sometimes came home early. He would immediately send the maid home, leading Margaret up the stairs and, without much conversation, unfasten the shirtwaist, pull up the skirt and push her down on the bed or onto an armchair. Feeling rushed, she objected. The more she objected, the less patient he became. Soon she learned that if she went along quietly, it would all be over quickly. When she became pregnant, the sex became more forceful. After both pregnancies ended in miscarriages, he lost interest in her altogether, choosing to satisfy himself elsewhere. These thoughts floated like dry leaves in her mind as she prepared for the annual Bankers Association Ball.

"Talley, I think I'll wear the emerald silk tonight," she said to her maid. The girl had been with her since she was thirteen and knew instinctively which dress Margaret would wear. "Yes, ma'am. I've laid it out for you." Margaret added a few drops of the elixir to her tea as she put the finishing touches on her face. She was late coming downstairs and their arrival at the party was barely noticed. A sullen Henry disappeared with a sturdy glass of whiskey soon afterward.

She was amazed by the energy she had that evening. She danced with Henry's associates until she began to feel dizzy. But where was he? Looking around the room, she caught sight of him leaning into a dark alcove with a young woman she had never seen before. He lingered.

Well, if that was the way it was to be, maybe she would find a distraction for herself. Her use of the potent tonic increased and after a few months she began to behave differently. She muttered to herself constantly, her voice only a raspy whisper.

Henry became impatient with her forgetfulness, noting her general lack of interest in her appearance or in whether he came home at all. She had become difficult, even embarrassing, on the rare occasions when they went out to parties. The recent ball had been an important event for him. Her nervous chatter and clumsy behavior had been so disruptive he insisted they leave the gala early. She was dragging him down, he thought, and the cost of her medicine was beyond reason.

He had involved himself more deeply in the weekly

poker game at the club. As a result, his debts had been mounting, and they would be difficult to pay off from Margaret's monthly draw from the trust and his salary alone. If she had not gotten into this situation it wouldn't have been a problem, he told his friends.

Dr. McNallie's Health Elixir for Women was increasingly helpful to Margaret and although expensive, not a day went by when she did not add it to her afternoon tea and indulge in a dose again after dinner.

Weeks after the Bankers Ball her hands were shaking and her vision blurry. She needed a dose of the elixir to help her face the day. Her supply usually lasted three weeks, but it had only been eight days and now she realized the bottle was empty. In desperation, she sent for the doctor, when the driver returned saying the doctor couldn't come, she rode the buggy down to the surgeon's office and sent the driver away. The heat of the day was rising and in the dust she struggled to breathe. The nurse took her to the examining room right away.

The surgeon generally insisted he see his patients when he filled the prescribed tonic to make sure of its effects. He was shocked to see Margaret's condition when she arrived. Perhaps the strength of the laudanum had changed since the last shipment. He had increased the dosage *only slightly*, he thought. The dark circles under her wild eyes gave her the look of a hunted animal. When he told her the next shipment of elixir would not arrive until the next day, she shrieked and smashed a glass beaker onto the floor as she ran past him and into the yard.

She collapsed outside the back door just as Sam Wah was unloading the new shipment of laudanum from the buckboard. He had just pulled a canvas tarp away from the corner of the wagon revealing its contents—a dozen wooden crates filled with straw and small bottles. He looked up to see the woman burst out of the door and sprawl headlong onto the dirt path of the rear entrance. He ran over to help her up, but she had lost consciousness.

Dr. McNallie was clearly rattled when he saw Sam kneeling over the woman. His face was red and his brow wet with perspiration. He checked her ragged breathing, and then turning to Sam, he shouted as he scooped up several bottles and dropped them into the pockets of his gray lab coat.

"Unload a case and take the rest of it up to my home on the ridge—you must go *NOW*. When you've unloaded the shipment, come back here. I will need you to take her home."

The surgeon looked deranged, with his hair standing out on end, the permanent vertical lines between his brows deeper than ever. Sam did what he was told to do. He wondered at the absurdity of the situation, but he wanted to get the shipment out of his wagon as soon as he could. It would take some time to get back to the clinic, he would have to pick up Ida at the store on his way. After stocking shelves all day and helping customers, she would be tired, but he knew he could count on her patience. The heat of the afternoon was rising.

Chief Ottinger

Before he accepted the offer to become police chief, George Hershal Ottinger had been informed of the need to "clean things up" in the city. That could mean many things, he knew. Graft and corruption were commonplace. What about bribery? Violent crime, obviously.

However, as the table of finely suited men pulled on their after-dinner cigars and released a variety of smoke rings, creating a cloud of pungent smoke. It became clear they were talking about "the vermin" infiltrating their good city, starting businesses, seeking to own property, making employment available to former slaves. The audacity of it all.

They had seen the growth of an unsavory element in other cities and watched as the power dynamic had changed. Growth had to be controlled, they agreed. They had created this city after all, it was theirs. Chief Ottinger came to understand that evening exactly the kind of community he would attempt to keep in check. One that had been arranged for the profit of these men.

He would maintain close ties with them, become their confidant, as much as they would allow. He would follow their directives in the smallest detail.

This did not mean he wouldn't appear to be friendly. He knew he would fare better if everyone thought he was on their side, smiling and quipping through his big pearly teeth—his greatest asset.

Upon accepting the offer, he wrote an eloquent speech, designed just for them. He delivered it on the day it was announced he would take office.

"I will make this promise to all, we will not tolerate vagrants and deviants, rogues and reprobates, nor any kind of vice. Some will never belong here and the people will watch and judge."

Sam and Ida

A day begins like any other day with some expression of light, an awakening of birds and an attitude of anticipation or dread. Thin layers of apprehension may build for many days until the pressure reaches a feverish pitch. Or everything seems sunny and fine, until it doesn't.

Like a shadow following Sam and Ida, the misdeeds of the greedy crept behind them. While it seemed like a normal day, panic had seized the surgeon, everyone seemed to be conspiring against him.

After he had sent his patients home, he tried to organize his thoughts. He needed to speak to Chief Ottinger before things got out of hand. Which, he could tell, they quickly were.

The heat of the day had become almost unbearable. Even though the surgeon's house was on the more accessible end of the ridge, Sam's mule was working hard to pull the cart up the long grade. Flecks of foam dropped from the animal's mouth. When they finally reached the house of the surgeon, the housekeeper had Sam carry the boxes of laudanum down two flights of stairs. When Sam was finished, he shut the door of the lower room and left the house. After watering the mule, he set off back down the Mission Ridge Road, stopping at the store to pick up Ida before heading to the clinic.

Dr. McNallie had revived the Montaigne woman long enough to give her a hastily mixed dose of the elixir and though she seemed dazed, she was able to walk to the wagon and lay on a pallet of quilts as they continued up the hill, this time toward her home. The skies were darkening in the distance and the air was becoming difficult to breathe. The surgeon summoned the police chief and spoke to him for a long time.

Sam watered the mule and adjusted the harness before they started up Cameron Lane. He noted the dark bank of clouds looming from the northwest.

"What is wrong with her?" asked Ida.

"I'm not sure, but it might have something to do with the crates I've been unloading. The doctor didn't want them at the office anymore."

When Sam's wagon rolled up the driveway at the Montaigne house, the sky had turned a sickly yellow green, filled with dust from a quickening wind. No one seemed to be around, so Sam carried Margaret into the house through the open front door with Ida trailing behind them, holding the woman's shawl. He carried her down the entry hall and under a broad arch into the elegant parlor, where he laid the sleeping figure on the divan. He placed the bottle of Dr. McNallie's elixir on a nearby table. They left the way they came, though the front door.

When Sam and Ida left the Montaigne's house, the first flashes of heat lightning lit up the sky. Before long, the jagged veins of ground lightning were followed seconds later by a crack of thunder. At last, large drops of rain, sparse at first, then forming a thick curtain. Thunder rolled and seven riders in dark clothing waited at the corner of High Road and Cameron Lane. The horses stamped nervously in the volatile atmosphere.

On the back side of Cameron Hill, just above the riverbank and the hollow, there was a forgotten swath of woodland where bobcats stalked rodents and small game. The area had never been denuded, even throughout the war. One could spot cougars sunning on rocky outcroppings early in the morning. It was a wild tangle of foliage studded with limestone boulders, overarched by giant old-growth hardwoods that had somehow survived the decimation of the war. Oak, chestnut, hickory, and poplar grew larger here than in any other region in this thick tangle of vines and trees beside the deep water.

That night, the owls were hunting along the riverside near the desolate stretch of road. Sam and Ida travelled, slowly and loosely reined, giving the mule his head. The riders waited until the wagon made the turn to Blue Goose

Hollow. Then they quietly followed, their furtive silhou-ettes dim in the gathering gloom.

Among those riding after Sam Wah and his wife that night was a man with a big mustache. In the heavy down-pour it was dripping at its ends which protruded outside the protection of his fedora. A trickle of brown liquid from the chew of tobacco he clenched in his big teeth mingled with the rainwater as it ran down his chin. He fastened a coil of rope with the saddle strings below the cantle of the saddle and handed another coil to the rider next to him. None of them spoke a word as the storm rose in intensity.

The tumult of the storm was such that neither Sam nor Ida heard the riders until it was too late. Not that they could have outrun them. They were trying to stay dry un-der a remnant of waxed canvas they used to cover grocery shipments.

Thunder crashed overhead and lightning struck a tree in the distance. The tree splintered and burst into flames; the spent mule barely raised his head. The wind pulled at the tarp and rain sprayed Sam and Ida's faces. They huddled closer. Sam took Ida's trembling hand in his. His long thin fingers intertwined with hers. She was afraid and although no one could hear her, she began humming. Just an old lullaby her aunt used to sing.

Without warning, a dark shape pulled up to one side of the exhausted mule, a rider grabbing the animal's harness. From behind, Sam and Ida were jerked down into the wagon well. The last thing either of them saw was a white patch of cloth as a hand closed over their faces. They smelled a strong and vaguely familiar odor before the blackness came.

CHAPTER NINE

1995

Russell

WALKING DOWN THE hall of the humanities building, Professor Bowers passed the wall of photographs of the early days at the landing. Rustic storefronts, shots of great train engines spewing steam. There were also full-figure military portraits of a few generals, both Confederate and Union. As he climbed the stairs to the second floor of the new library, the photographs became more recent. The faces of the august Fellowship of Southern Writers greeted him. Black and white portraits of Eudora Welty, Robert Penn Warren, Shelby Foote, Ernest Gaines, and two dozen other great talents peered at him seriously, as though daring him to guess their darkest secrets. The collective works of these writers illustrated the backbone of modern southern culture. Russell couldn't help but wonder what he didn't know—how astounding the undocumented times might have been. What other events had been completely overlooked?

He was interested in the photographs Vivienne had found. He stopped to chat for a few minutes with Rachel Johnson, the processing archivist, showing her the photos of the house and the Chinese laborers. Her office walls were filled with incredible images from various periods in local history. There was a photo of FDR in his historic modified motorcar with its top down at the Chickamauga Dam. A photo of the city's oldest bridge, its early buildings and fountains. The university was deeply connected to all the city's history, ever since its founding. And Rachel was the keeper of that history.

"These are amazing, Russell," she said, emphasizing each word individually as she examined the photographs with great interest. "The old wall has been around for a long time and although you'd never know, it has been the backdrop for plenty of drama. But that's the thing about place—a place is not just a location, it's a place in time. And that makes it unique.

"On the fourth floor you'll find a restricted collection of archival material. There are several articles you need to read. Take your time." She handed him a yellow legal sheet with titles and references scribbled down.

"Thanks, Rachel," he said as he continued down the hallway.

"Hey, stop by and give your regards to Jim McDuffie, on the way. Just a few more days."

"Wow, I almost forgot—that's the other reason I came!"

Jim had been the head librarian for close to forty years, practically an institution himself. He had degrees in library science and antiquities and had helped the university library assemble a large collection of regional books and artifacts over his many years there. He often travelled for speeches and workshops—his dry humor creating almost a cult following. Who would ever be able to replace him?

Russell heard a commotion in the library's community room. The double doors were open and there was McDuffie, in his characteristic bow tie and white shirt, munching on cake with pink and green icing and laughing at something said by one among the half-circle of friends and colleagues surrounding him.

"Possibly," Jim said, "but finding the Twain-Tesla correspondence was probably the highlight. You never know what you'll find, always in the most unlikely places." With that, Jim turned and greeted Russell.

"Glad you could make it, my friend."

The son of a Presbyterian minister from North Carolina, Jim was replete with stories from his life. At eighty-two, he enjoyed sharing them. The more time Russell spent with him, the bolder and more colorful Jim's stories became. He could talk to anyone on a variety of subjects. His experience was deep, his understanding and broad knowledge were more experiential than bookish.

Once, Russell had heard him discussing flowers with the neighborhood homeless man, Sandy, who picked wildflowers and sold them to people on the street. He was also allowed to pick from certain summer gardens for special customers. McDuffie would occasionally order a bouquet from Sandy for a staff breakfast. He always came through.

Jim had also been known to engage a popular local attorney, who was an avid bird hunter, in telling colorful stories about their hunting dogs. Each man would try to outdo the other in descriptions of how smart their dogs were. The tales only grew taller.

"Why, Jake went to fetch the mail the other day," said Jim. "It took longer than usual. I wondered what happened until I looked out the window. There he was, down by the mailbox. He'd fetched the mail all right, and he was reading it, too!"

All told, McDuffie had doubled the community use of the library and tripled the engagement of the faculty and students through his natural gift of outreach. Over the many years he had been head university librarian, book titles in all genres of the collection had increased by over sixty percent.

Only a couple of blocks from the university library was the historic Carnegie Library. It was built in 1905 and it was one of hundreds built across the nation by business-man and steel magnate, Andrew Carnegie. Russell took the elevator up to the next floor and was greeted by a western view of the Carnegie Library roofline when he stepped out. He began pulling the information Rachel had suggested.

Many of the articles and anecdotes had been transferred to new digital media, yet by pulling the bound annual volumes of newspapers from the library shelves, he came across obscure clippings describing almost every trifling event since the War. It was a time of high energy and intense drama. From the flooding of the river to the building of the wall; from the yellow fever epidemic to prohibition, Russell refreshed what he already knew and discovered a few anecdotes that he had never heard before.

Flood, Fever, and Folly, 1867—Robert Handman

Almost ten years before the yellow fever epidemic there was an epic flood. On March fourth as the area was reeling in the aftermath of the war, it began to rain. For five days, heavy rains poured throughout the length of the great river valley, including the entire watershed for many miles upriver. By the time it stopped, the streets of the city were under eight feet of water and the river had crested at fifty-eight feet. If there had been a record, it would surely have been record-breaking. Certainly, in the memories of the five thousand people who lived in the area, it was so.

Low-lying croplands and pastures were washed out. There was vast structural damage, the most obvious being that the military bridge was swept away. Homes and businesses along the shore and in low-lying areas were demolished. The trains that gave the city its identity were not running, and the telegraph lines were eventually downed. Communication lost. The higher ground of Mission Ridge and Cameron Hill, Fort Wood, and the new military cemetery—all were unreachable, and the dirt tracks of Market and Broad Street were turned to cold rivers of mud.

Two days after the rain began the local sawmill owner, Robert Handman, saddled his horse, Molly, and rode into town. He was to meet a buyer at the Crutchfield Hotel about a shipment of logs. Stabling the mare on the side street, Handman walked into the hotel lobby with his paperwork, hoping to close the deal for delivery. Crossing the lobby, he noticed people scurrying out from the lead crystal doors of the restaurant. Inside he saw at least six inches of water standing on the floor in the back and the water was aggressively rising. The maître d' tugged at his watch fob and studied the time, nervously waiting for a table of businessmen to finish, so he could close the restaurant and go home. At the desk, Handman learned that his business contact had checked out, so he walked the two short blocks to his riverfront mill office where he found absolutely no one at all working.

The employees who were there had gathered under a tin awning on the dock in a sudden downpour to watch a group of men curiously standing on the bridge above them and about two hundred yards upstream. He called to John Portman, his foreman, a thoughtful man who had an easy way with people and the confidence of the mill employees.

"John, we should be securing the building, the lower floor will surely flood," he shouted through the wind and spitting rain.

"It's a problem of communication, Robert. The noise of the storm—we can't be heard above it," Portman answered. "We'll get to it right now." Suddenly there was a loud, wrenching screech and they turned to watch the enormous steel girders on the far side of the river twist and break away from the shore. The wooden beams splintered, some of them crashing into the river. The massive shudder sent the men who were examining the bridge on the south end plunging into the cold gray water. Even though the bridge was little more than a year old, the piers at the north shore were known to be on softer footing and less stable. The terrified cries of the men in the water were almost drowned out by the sound of the wind and rain.

"Quick, let's get the rowing skiff," barked Handman. He jumped into the boat with Portman, and they rowed out nearly to where the current was gushing round the bend. Throwing a rope tied to a two-foot cable spool to the first head that bobbed up, Handman knelt in the boat while the oarsman kept it as steady as possible. The first man latched on and was pulled into the boat. Several of the fallen had grabbed the scrubby growth emerging from the boiling surf and one by one they were plucked like kittens from trees and hauled safely back to the dock of the mill. Their tweed suits and full beards were heavy and dripping as they absorbed their close-call in stunned silence. Handman and his foreman were the heroes of the day.

The mill workmen stayed as long as they dared, barricading windows and bagging valuables until a great swell loosened a huge raft of logs and swept them out with the current, crashing into the corner of the millhouse itself. Each man scattered in his own direction. When they had all left for their homes, Handman ran down the street to fetch his horse.

Many of the stables were built, tucked into the side of the hill near the riverbank, out of sight from traffic on the street. The horse was in one of these.

By the time he reached her, Molly was in a state, snorting and screaming as the water rose up to her withers. Though the water was chest high, Handman negotiated the lower aisle in front of the stalls by holding onto the row of bars. Opening the stall door enough to get through, he got the bridle back on the horse, and practically swimming onto her back he pushed the door open further, preparing to head out of the barn, leaving saddle and pad behind. "Let's go, Moll," he said. The horse squeezed into the aisle and swam the length of it, then scrambled up the ramp and out onto the street.

The cobbles of Chestnut Street clattered loudly as Molly trotted, shaking and snorting indignantly, eyes rolling, with Handman clinging to her as they headed home. The air was cold, but the rain had temporarily stopped. Along the banks in the growing darkness, he could hear faint cries from the river, where he knew all manner of shanties and coops, buggies and boxes filled with animals and people clinging to their belongings were being washed downriver in the torrent.

These people, he wondered, *how much can they endure?* As if war, pestilence, and famine were not sufficient on all sides, now this calamity. He would end up abandoning his own home the next day as the floodwaters swelled.

It was later rumored that whole families had drowned. Although the exact death toll was unknown, corpses of animals and men floated through the city's flooded streets for days. Rumor was the main format for information, but the newspapers made a valiant effort to get the facts.

The Daily Times was the primary newspaper of the day. Later, it would be owned by a young publishing entrepreneur with integrity and an abundance of ambition. The newspaperman would become highly successful and his rise to grandeur would come out of a stubborn focus resulting in an almost "mythological rags-to-riches story," according to later newspaper accounts. His reputation would help him years later with New York City bankers when he purchased the financially faltering New York

Times for $75,000 in 1896. By 1900 the paper was showing consistent profits.

Yet, in the city at the time of the flood, The Daily Times reported all the facts it could gather, including colorful incidents like the deliverance of farmer Albert Kesterton from the 450-acre island below the lost bridge, who escaped by holding onto the horns of his favorite heifer as she swam to the opposite shore. Since the Native American removal, the island in the middle of the great river—Williams Island—had been farmed, but during a flood it had to be evacuated and that included removing cattle, horses, and mules. The wagons, tools, feed, and supplies were lost.

The 1867 flood stalled efforts toward war reconstruction and it would be many years before a new bridge would be built. Almost eighty years later, the written accounts of the flood would inspire officials to propose a series of dams to tame the river. There were dozens of studies and cost reports. It took years of planning and negotiating with federal and state officials and the United States Congress to approve and begin such a colossal project.

Yellow Fever, 1878 — Thomas Carlisle

Thomas Carlisle, a major in the Union army, had been serving as a quartermaster in the city near the end of the war. This conquered area was scattered with remnants of troop encampments, burned homesteads and denuded forestland, but it still retained a natural beauty created by the river and the surrounding mountains. He kept detailed diaries and descriptions of his service in the region.

One of his duties before the war officially ended was the oversight and provisions for the few prisoners that remained at an encampment on Lookout Creek, miles above where it emptied into the Tennessee. He was awaiting orders as to what should become of them, when the region was engulfed in a vacuous wave of cold from the northwest and temperatures dipped to fifteen degrees below zero for several consecutive nights. The creek was frozen a foot deep in some places.

Touring the camp alone during the week, he came upon a couple of Union soldiers standing guard over a wretched pair of men in tattered grays, who were out by the creekbank for some exercise, as the sunshine had recently returned. The men looked old beyond their years, but one, Confederate Private Alfred Joe Peters, was only seventeen. He was moving along the surface of the creek in his work boots—not military issue, since by the time he enlisted there weren't any more. These had been his father's shoes.

Alfred Joe kept falling, unable to navigate the phenomenal ice. He was yelling wildly about how he had never seen a frozen river and his northern guards were laughing uproariously. He was trying to get back to the creekbank, but the more he tried, the more he lost control, his feet spinning as he flew backwards. Arms flailing, he pulled himself up and tried again to the amusement of those watching. Further and further downstream he proceeded until, not laughing any more, they lost sight of him around the creek's bend.

"The simple fool's gone," said the sergeant. Rifles in hand, they sprang off through the snowy woods after him, anticipating he would emerge along the bank. But Alfred Joe was a mile down the frozen creek, gliding smoothly on the ice and heading home.

The cold air burned his lungs, and his feet were numb as he scanned the creek side for the memorable spot he was looking for—his favorite fishing hole. Soon he saw the clay-colored ribbon of the bank, the notch in the creek where the water pooled, so cool in the summer with the blue mountain rising behind it. Frozen now, it was still so familiar. He climbed up the bank and from there he set off across a field of tall silver grass in the direction of his family's farm, nearly seven miles away.

Alfred Joe crossed two large farms on the way, both now with the main farmhouses and barns burned to the ground. Some of the outer buildings were still standing and it looked as though a few people had been living in what had been a smokehouse. He came across a couple of warm eggs in a forgotten coop and ate them raw. Struggling to refocus his mind and ignore the bitter cold, he thought of dappled sunshine playing across the tin roof of an earlier chicken house and remembered gathering eggs on a summer day years before with his old friend, Joshua Crutchfield. The freckle-faced boy of his childhood was eager for any adventure and could turn simple chores into entertaining diversions. He was just a memory now. Private Crutchfield had been shot in the face at Chickamauga.

In a few years Alfred Joe's large farm would be traded for another parcel of land so a national military park could be created to memorialize the war dead, fallen at the site. He stretched his stiff back as he stood up and after a parting look around, set off again. He would be the last war prisoner in the area to escape.

Tired of war and fighting, Carlisle recorded the sketch in his diary, simply concluding at the end never to underestimate a farmer. The remaining days of the conflict were uneventful in the valley and there would be no more wartime entries.

Carlisle, who was originally from Pennsylvania, saw potential in the river landing. There was not much of a real village here to speak of, but he was a visionary and hopeful, imagining the city as it surely would become. Upon his discharge, he decided to bring his wife and children from their home in Philadelphia to make a life here. The bloom of prosperity immediately after the war's end was exciting. Over the next decade he became deeply involved with the Alabama Great Southern Railroad. Described as mild-mannered and gentlemanly, he was successful in his business dealings and determined to see the city grow. During that time, he was elected alderman for seven consecutive terms.

Friends suggested he run for mayor and in October of 1877 he was elected for a one-year term. He was handsome, hopeful, and positive, expressing his interest in education and the economy in his inaugural speech. The town was openly inviting people to move to the newly expanding community on the banks of the river. Ads touting the beauty and richness of the region had been placed by the city's two, major law firms and they made the possibilities seem endless, although not without challenge.

There was still plenty of trouble in the world. Like a roll of thunder in the distance, the

Caribbean islands were being ravaged by yellow fever in the early months of 1878. United States President Rutherford Hayes signed the Quarantine Act to prevent the spread of the fever to the southern states. Sadly, despite the new law, and although it was believed to be disease-free, a ship out of Havana was allowed to enter the port of New Orleans. From there, travelers and mosquitoes helped spread the disease up the Mississippi River Valley to Memphis. Once the fever was raging there, refugees began to pour out in all directions, especially east, into the city.

Mayor Carlisle and the town council were not idle that summer. In July, they passed a law to restrict animals, both wild and domestic, from roaming the streets and appropriated funds to clean the sewers. Carlisle created a Citizens' Relief Committee to work with refugees. Their efforts were valiant, in fact, but the fever was becoming so widespread that the board of aldermen discontinued its regular meetings to curtail the infection.

While many left the city to escape the illness, Carlisle remained and worked among the sick, exhibiting the strength of his remarkable character. If only strength of character had been enough to save him. Mayor Carlisle contracted yellow fever and died in late October, the last person in the city to die from the disease — almost one year to the day he took office. He was buried in what would become the National Cemetery—the first military cemetery to be established in the entire United States. Major George Henry Thomas, who became an early investor in the Coca-Cola Bottling Company, had ordered the appropriation of seventy-five acres of land to inter Union soldiers, many of whom had fallen in combat on nearby battlefields. As early as 1870 there were 12,000 interments, most of whom were unknown.

Russell read through these accounts one by one, imagining the characters and how they came to be victims or heroes of the time. He was good at reading between the lines and could visualize them from the anecdotes. Their stories were an important legacy of their time if they were known. So many stories had been lost.

CHAPTER TEN

1995
Maddie

MADDIE UNLOADED A bag of groceries, mostly snacks—cheeses, cherries, cashews. Russell came in a few minutes later, his shirt almost untucked, his hair windblown. Tossing his satchel down in a chair he began a familiar rant, but one she had not heard in a long time.

"Why is the impact of human folly always compounded by natural occurrences?" Russell asked. Some historic events were the results of disease and natural disaster. "Slavery, the native removal, the ravages of war and the crippling pollution brought on by the advent of heavy industry in the valley—were all manmade problems," Russell said. "I'm going to weave that thought into my presentation tomorrow. Students need to consider the anonymous individuals who helped rebuild the region and the nation after each calamity.

"There were many, whether enslaved or free, who played important roles in making life better and their efforts were never acknowledged." He rummaged through his satchel for evidence and withdrew a folder. The photographs Russell held in his hand captured the essence of the Chinese workers of the late 1880s, their faces frozen in time. Here the men were at arm's length and simultaneously one hundred years away. One could touch the stones they had laid but could not touch them.

"This was a place in time." He waved the photos dramatically above his head. Maddie only grinned and shook her head. Was he trying to entertain her or was he seriously expressing his passion?

"I think I've been looking at it from the wrong perspective. It was a time of intense change, from medical discovery to industrial innovation. The rapid change heightened the opportunity for error and adaptation would require a change in actions and expectations," said Russell. Then he dropped into a deep, thoughtful funk.

The longer he taught history, the more intrigued with the concept of time he became. Once, he had believed that a society which studied and understood its mistakes would make fewer of them. Its people could avoid many disasters of their own making. He no longer entertained those notions. Time changed the ways people interacted with each other. Unfortunately, it did little to alter their base motivations.

History, Russell thought, why would anyone choose it? He thought of his son, who wanted nothing to do with his father's passion, not just studying history but teaching it. The subject only revealed the mistakes mankind would, in fact, continue to make. *Well, there was no way to get around the liability of being human.*

Maddie knew Russell indulged in this sort of thinking every now and then, until he remembered what he loved about it. The study of history was like working a giant floor puzzle. Things happened and there were clues as to why. Some pieces fit, others did not. The shadows of the past came together with the shapes of the present, creating colorful, sometimes joyous, but often troubling images. When viewed up close those images could be confusing. The observer had to stand back to really appreciate the complete picture.

Looking at the faces of the builders of the wall, their own mysterious home on the ridge in the background, he wondered how much those men had influenced their story.

"So, I take it you've been perusing the library archives this afternoon," said Maddie as she joined him at the table where he had laid out what few pieces he could take away.

"Yes, I couldn't believe I found anything relevant."

"Like what?" asked Maddie, with interest.

"Did you know this man was hanged on the bridge, with his wife, in the summer of 1890?" Russell asked, pointing to a grim clipping that showed a fuzzy image of the bodies hanging from the bridge. "I found a newspaper article that said they were responsible for drugging a woman on Cameron Hill. The woman died. And here he is again in our photograph of the builders."

"Really?" she said as she poured a bourbon. She took a few moments to scan the clipping. "Hanged from the bridge. A woman?"

"Right. It appears the justice system didn't have the opportunity to be involved."

He stood and absently shuffled the papers back into the folder. "What have you been doing this afternoon?"

"We got some shots of the house. You won't believe what I found out today about your brother. John Clark stopped by to drop off some papers. He said Gray tried to buy this place two years ago, but the owner wouldn't sell. Turns out, he was furious with John when he found out it came on the market. And that *we* bought it."

"Why does he care? He can get any house he wants. What is it about this one?"

"I don't know," said Maddie. "John says he had a verbal agreement with the widow who owned it, but she backed out before signing. I guess she thought her son wanted the property."

Russell didn't want to talk about his brother, but he was perpetually interested in whatever Maddie talked about. And like any good conversationalist, he had questions of his own. What would it have been like to live here when the house was first built? What aspects would be the same, what things would be different?

"Quieter, fewer neighbors," said Maddie. "Farther to go to buy good bourbon."

She leaned in and kissed him, and Russell decided to take the opportunity to make use of their child-free home and left dinner thawing on the counter while they slipped away to the bedroom.

Maddie dreamed that night of passing through an archway in a thick, stone wall. In her dream, she walked down a staircase that wound in irregular circles, now narrow, now swinging wide. The footing was loose, and she struggled to see in the dim light. At the bottom of the stairs, she turned to look back. A man stood on the landing; his white shirt luminous in the gloom of the chamber. Without warning, the stairway disappeared. The man on what was now a ledge offered her an outstretched hand. Maddie struggled to reach it; each time she got closer, he seemed further away. When she woke, her thin cotton nightshirt was drenched with sweat.

The next morning, she stepped out for a jog along the empty sidewalk of Crest Road. She was nothing if not habitual, and her custom was to take a morning run along the west face of the ridge, then cross over and run back along the lower east side, where the early morning sun was already uncomfortably warm. The street dipped low along the ridge into the shade of the trees, then rose again, adding elevation and distance, giving her route a little variety. It was the coolest time of day and commanded the most unique view of the valley, still in shadow. The run was far better than caffeine. It lifted her spirits and helped her come alive for the day.

As she crossed over the ridge and picked up the trail down to the lower street, she noticed a car pulling out of a side alley. It followed her for the next mile. The low rumble of the engine felt threateningly close, so Maddie glanced back and motioned for the driver to go around. After a minute or two, the car accelerated and blew past her. She couldn't make out the driver or remember more than the first three digits of the license tag. Nor did she recognize the vehicle, a late model sedan.

When Maddie burst into the kitchen, she was clearly rattled and breathing heavily as she told Russell about what had happened since she left the house. He put down his coffee cup.

"The car followed me almost the entire time," she choked back tears and took a long draft from her water bottle. "What can we do?"

"I'll call the detective who came to the Wheelhouse," Russell said. "Are you sure you didn't get more of the tag number?" She shook her head.

"At least I can give them a description of the car."

First the vandalism, now this. Maddie felt frantic, certain the two events weren't coincidental. She wrote down her account of the jogging incident and spent almost an hour talking to police detectives about it, although they said without the tag number there wasn't much they could do.

"I just can't think about this anymore," she told Russell that evening. "It's too exhausting." While the work on the roof continued, Maddie poured herself into refinishing the shelves and woodwork in the library. And following that, she organized her digital images of the project, room by room.

Fortunately for the roofers and deck installers, the dry weather held throughout the months of July and August. The morning sun rose in a haze of white heat that peaked at mid-afternoon. It set each night in an opulent blaze of cadmium orange.

During the high summer, a bustling team of workers pressure-washed the porches, patios, and walkways. Then they began on the stone walls of the house. Amid the commotion, Maddie and Russell scrubbed and painted the fireplaces. The new light fixtures arrived and were hung, after the re-wiring had been completed. Two of the fixtures had to be sent back, but eventually all arrived in good order. Crews came and went. The project was moving along, and every night, Maddie and Russell collapsed into bed from exhaustion. Day after day, alternating doses of ibuprofen, bottled water, iced coffee and the occasional spirit kept them going.

"Pizza," Maddie complained as Russell walked in and set the flat box on the counter. "Really?"

"Well, we've had Thai two nights in a row," Russell mumbled, swept up in an exhausted fog, which was rare for him. "I think the hot peppers are making me hallucinate. I thought I saw someone on the landing just now, but the floorboards are still all pulled up."

"What kind of someone?"

"I don't know," Russell said, opening a box and lifting a soggy slice. "I'm just tired. I'll make a pot of coffee."

Late one night in August, nearing the end of phase one, the full moon cast blue panes across the cotton bedsheet as Maddie fell into a fathomless sleep. She drifted once again down the dark circling staircase. This time, when she reached the bottom, she felt compelled to wait.

"Where is it?" Someone whispered in her ear. "Where is it?"

She could feel their hot breath on her neck. Bolting upright, she opened her eyes, but only a sleeping Russell lay next to her. Her senses heightened by the fright, she heard his steady breath, her own heart pounding in her chest and a strange sound coming from outside. She crossed the room to the window.

In the moonlight, Maddie could see shadows on the grass, cast by three figures at the end of the exterior wall. Before she could prod Russell into consciousness, they disappeared.

The next day, the work of the night visitors was obvious. Several feet of exterior wall had been covered with graffiti, similar to what had appeared on the Wheelhouse. The house on Mission Ridge wore its embellishment like a wound. It was angry, and it stayed that way until Maddie had the art sandblasted away.

Though Maddie didn't tell him about her dreams, she and Russell talked often about who had tagged their house. The Wheelhouse was an old commercial building now remade into an office center in a rundown part of town.

Graffiti was common there. But for the same vandals to make their way through the scrub and brush on the ridge just to target one specific house seemed too intentional. No one had a good explanation, and it was discouraging. The police seemed disinterested. Meanwhile, two different real estate agents had called, just to see if the house might be on the market again.

"Have you thought about the possibility of getting it into shape and just selling it?" Maddie asked one afternoon.

"I am not deterred," proclaimed Russell. "This house was meant for us."

He could be blindly stubborn, she thought, but always with a smile, and she loved that about him. But she had doubts about herself. *Could she see this through?*

Marion

The family weekend at the lake was a much-needed break for Maddie and Russell. It was an annual event. The lake house was normally used as a vacation rental, but Maddie and her sister Marion chose one weekend a year to meet there, since Marion lived near Knoxville. Their children were grown and off pursuing their own lives, so Maddie, Marion, and their husbands would enjoy some quiet time this year.

Marion's two younger brothers were always too busy to attend family weekend, or so they said. Now that their parents were gone, they weren't interested in the lake house. She had the feeling they would soon insist on selling it. More reason to enjoy it while she could.

Marion was a remarkable cook. She wrote a food column for a regional newspaper and was something of a celebrity chef, appearing at popular food festivals and the Sunday Summer Market for cooking demonstrations.

Italian food was her specialty. She had opened the Bluejay Trattoria a decade ago and recently sold it to an enterprising young couple with plenty of energy, a requirement for keeping a restaurant running. Marion shared with Maddie in their regular phone calls that she sometimes felt a tinge of seller's remorse but was happy to slow down.

As was tradition on lake weekends, Marion did the cooking, but Russell and Maddie supplied the ingredients. On Friday morning, they loaded the SUV with fresh tomatoes, mushrooms, onions and peppers, olive oil, two dozen eggs and plenty of fresh basil. They packed a cooler with the meat and seafood, then headed to the lake, stopping only to pick up wine and ice at the boathouse shop on the way. Crossing the Hiwassee River and climbing the wooded hills beyond, they turned down Ramblers Cove Road before reaching the rustic house at the end of the lane.

Marion's husband, Gil, arrived next, along with their homemade pasta, fresh smoked mozzarella, parmesan cheese and a delightful, locally sourced pancetta. And, just in time for an afternoon swim, Marion pulled up in her bright yellow station wagon, late because of a cooking demonstration she presented at what was probably the only bistro in three outlying counties.

As the sisters embraced, did Marion imagine it, or did Maddie look a bit harried? Those dark circles under her eyes suggested weariness uncharacteristic of her energetic sibling.

"What's up, Maddie?" Marion asked. "Ready for the weekend?"

"More than ready! I've been a little stressed out lately, with work and the house and all that goes with it."

Maddie didn't want to reveal the recent vandalism, not to mention her lack of sleep due to troublesome dreams. She didn't think her sister would want to hear it. Marion was easy-going and uncomplicated. She pursued what she loved, enjoyed the product of her labors, and lived well. She had long ago given up her anxiety over dietary restrictions. She had a fuller figure than her sister and tended to wear clothes that were colorful and vibrant, unlike Maddie's collection of cool neutrals. Marion was naturally pretty, and her aura was one of happiness which translated into a lush beauty.

After unpacking the cars, the foursome cooled off with a swim where a rocky outcropping dropped to the surface of the lake. Then, they spent the rest of the afternoon on the boat, a thirty-one-foot Beneteau First 300 Spirit—Gil's newest love.

He had found the boat in Florida and sailed it around the Gulf of Mexico for a while before shipping it home. It was unusual for the region. The strait bow and hard chine of the French sailboat made it distinctive, both in appearance and performance.

Cruising the bay at a mellow speed, the windswept blue surface of the water banished the oppressive humidity. They tacked back and forth up to the very end of the bay before coming round, and with the wind behind them, lightly floated back down again. The late afternoon wind would be good for only two or three hours this time of year, but it was worth the effort.

Bonnet the terrier, outfitted with her life vest, was bouncing back and forth from stern to bow. Her excitement was comical until she missed her landing and almost plunged into the water. Maddie reached out and grabbed the handle of her vest before she went over the edge as the boat swung around. Otherwise, the cruise was uneventful.

Gil skippered with a relaxed pride, pleased to be on the water. Blue herons waded in the small bays, unbothered by the boat's passing. Ospreys flew overhead to their nests atop defoliated trees and power poles. As the sailboat glided near the highway bridge, the mud nests of swallows could be seen lining the underside.

The area was bio-diverse, with hundreds of species of fish, reptiles, amphibians, and birds known to either inhabit the lake or migrate through. Over 120 species of mussels alone lived in the streams that fed the lake. They were a big part of the state's economy, harvested and exported around the world for growing freshwater pearls—the chips of the mussel shells were planted in oysters to create an irritation, and then a lovely pearl. Some of these mussels, a few of the mammalian species, and especially the bat populations were at risk in the changing environment. Although, a look around told Maddie that the entire habitat was in jeopardy.

They had been enjoying the lake house for years. With only five houses and a couple of rustic cabins strewn across the eastern shore, the long bay was never overcrowded. Yet, a new gated development was underway along the meadows of the north end, where sandhill cranes landed in large flocks every winter. The birds, whose numbers were making a comeback after years of decline, seemed to require the length of a football field to land. Usually landing in the meadows in January with their necks stretched out and their long legs trailing behind them, the migrating flocks ranged on the lake's system of islands, their loud clattering calls echoing across the water.

Sandhill cranes mated for life and instinctively returned to the same area to nest each year. After hatching, the gangly little birds were ready to fly the next day. But an accommodating habitat was key to their survival and the commercial development of their nesting areas interfered.

From the boat, the view of the water was dazzling. As they sailed closer to shore, they could see cement mixers alongside oversized foundations extending almost to the water's edge, where a one-hundred-year-old willow stood like a wise old woman with her feet in the water. The fate of the old tree was unclear. A debate raged on as to whether the tree would be removed.

Maddie thought gated developments were revolting, and this one was particularly offensive. She had written letters, signed petitions, and shown up at community meetings, but the new property owner had connections in Nashville and the deal was too far along to change. The complaints fell on deaf ears, the same way calls for environmental stewardship always did.

When they docked, the summer sun had dipped below the water and the owls had come out to hunt. Russell popped the cork on a nice prosecco while Marion assembled a Caesar salad, served with anchovy fritters, followed by grilled prawns the size of her hand, tossed in a sea of tomatoes, shallots, and basil. Later they enjoyed Marion's classic tiramisu.

The quick chatter of a family starved for news of each other led down one path, then another one. Some families played games. They weren't a family of card players, but they were fabulous storytellers. Marion was a master who could take a simple anecdote and embellish it beyond recognition. Tonight, she told the story of a friend's new restaurant opening with all the celebrity guests, it was as though they were characters on a stage.

Sometime between dinner and dessert Russell and Maddie began sharing stories about the renovation of the house on Mission Ridge, including its problems.

"Nothing has been stolen, so the police don't seem to care," Russell said.

"Maybe they just have too much going on to care about graffiti and broken windows. At any rate, we've installed security cameras at both the Wheelhouse and at home, at least until the work is finished. The security service starts on Monday, so, maybe it will help."

"Sure, it will," Gil declared, between a bite of tiramisu and a sip of coffee. Marion was horrified by the jogging incident and insisted on giving Maddie three cans of mace from the stash she kept in her car. Maddie had no idea Marion was so paranoid, but she agreed to one slender can of mace. It was attached to a cord with a carabiner on the end, so she could carry it easily on her jogs.

The next morning dawned lazy and serene. Maddie and Marion hiked to a mostly forgotten fire tower on the hill above the lake house and climbed six flights of rusted stairs to the lookout on top. Surveying the blue-green panorama all around them created a familiar nostalgia.

"Remember when we came up here for picnics with the cousins?" asked Maddie "It's remarkable that nobody fell."

"It was fun, but a little easier to climb in those days," Marion puffed as she reached the top. Maddie had brought along binoculars, and she used them to scan the blue hills. She could see a hot air balloon floating far down the reservoir, over the dam and miles upriver from the city bridges. For a moment, she was transported to an earlier summer, when she and Russell had taken the children to a balloon festival, a colorful and in many ways simpler time in their lives.

"I'm sorry you're having trouble with the house, is there anything I can do?" said Marion. "It all sounds pretty creepy."

"You're doing it now," Maddie said. In fact, she did feel refreshed just by being away from the work. The landscape was restful, the hopeful sky a China blue, delicate clouds in the distance.

They spent the rest of the day at the lake, alternating between lounge chairs on the shore and lime green plastic tubes in the clear, cool water. Everyone had acquired a deeper skin color by evening, except for the carefully screened Russell, who wouldn't let his ginger complexion make him miss a moment of the fun. Rather, he layered a safari hat, heavy sunscreen and sunglasses over a white long-sleeved shirt and rolled up khakis.

"What?" he had remarked that morning as Maddie raised an eyebrow. "I look stunning?"

"Something like that," Maddie teased.

They said their goodbyes the next day, vowing to get together again when the renovation on the Mission Ridge house was complete.

As Maddie and Russell drove home, a summer thunderstorm looked for a low place on the ridge to pass through and caught them just as they made the north crest. Ground lightning flashed. The rain mixed with pellets of hale that pounded the roof of the car so loudly they couldn't speak above it. But the turbulence of the weather was no match for the horror they felt when they walked through the front door.

Russell

"Sweet Jesus," Russell yelled, turning instinctively to block Maddie from entering. She hadn't heard him over the rain and came barreling into the front hall, screaming when she saw the dead cat. It was nailed to the wall, up-side-down like the Apostle Peter, its throat slit, blood dripping down the wall.

The smell was overwhelming.

Officers Howell and Gomez checked the house for intruders. Finding none, they began the assembly of details for their report—a broken kitchen window with traces of blood, the bloody tracks of a tennis shoe. They estimated the time of the break-in to be Friday evening and had Maddie and Russell check for valuables that might have been stolen. None were.

After the police left, Russell nailed a piece of plywood over the kitchen window.

"Should we get a hotel room?" he asked.

"No!" Maddie said, angrily. "I'm not going anywhere."

She thought about the nine-millimeter Ruger still in her bedside table. Small comfort. It was a sleepless night, the heat was sweltering and her dreams were filled with fragments of scenes from the house. Two days later, Officer Howell called to say he had very little information.

"We ran the blood sample and partial fingerprints through the system, but no matches," he said. "Although he hasn't shown up in our system, whoever did this is a nasty piece of work and you should be careful."

The cleanup was sluggish and hampered by their fatigue which was more emotional than physical. The window replacement had to be ordered and was slow to arrive. The tile was steam cleaned to remove the dried blood. Everything they tried to accomplish seemed tedious.

Maddie kept going over the details of the past weeks.

Who would be cruel enough to do something like that? Nothing seemed to fit.

"We need a break," she sighed. "For now—the work has to come to a halt."

Zee

Zee stopped by one afternoon to observe the renovations, up close. She was delighted to find Maddie had her favorites—pistachios and port—ready on a wicker tray.

Summer's oppressive heat had finally softened, and the two women sat on the rear veranda under the lazy rotation of a fan the size of an aircraft engine. Bonnet made herself comfortable on her mat, nearby.

"It's a beautiful spot," said Zee, as she gazed out over the valley toward the distant blue foothills of the Great Smokies. It was a clear day with a hint of a breeze. "Do you know about the missionaries who travelled to the Chickamauga Mission, just out there, to the east?" Zee pointed to a low expanse of rooftops beside a narrow stand of trees in the middle distance.

"Russell has mentioned it, but I don't remember much," Maddie said. She was starting to relax again, with the house projects behind her. The late seasonal sounds lulled her—the cawing of crows squabbling over the chokeberries on the hillside. A red-tailed hawk screaming, shrilly, as it soared on the wind, high overhead.

"They crossed the ridge near here," Zee said. "Established the mission in 1817 and educated about 300 students over twenty years. Not long after it opened, it was renamed the Brainerd Mission after David Brainerd. He was a Yale educated minister in the 1740s, who spent the last few years of his young life teaching Delaware

Indian children to speak English and attempting to convert them to Christianity, with only limited success."

"So, he died young?" asked Maddie.

"Yes, tuberculosis at twenty-nine. He never even visited this area. The only thing left of the mission now is the cemetery. You see where those trees are?" Again, Zee gestured to the east. "Jonathan Edwards wrote a popular biography of Brainerd after he died. That's probably the only reason anyone even remembers his name."

"Mmm," said Maddie, her thoughts wandering. Sometimes names just stick. Did the house have a name? She hushed her runaway thoughts long enough to respond. "That's the value of good publicity, I suppose."

"Or the value of a good friend," Zee winked. She took in a long view of the freshly painted porch and let out a contented sigh. "The house is stunning, Maddie."

"I must give Russell the credit, he has approached the project creatively and had much more fortitude than I have. His love of history flourishes here."

The month of September had given them cooler weather and a little peace—they were ready to celebrate what had been accomplished if they could just keep the vandals at bay.

"Now that the major improvements have almost been finalized, we're planning a little party next week to celebrate," said Maddie. "Just a few friends. Can you come?"

"I wouldn't miss it!" Zee replied with a sly smile. "Who's catering?"

Maddie

Maddie was born into a large family of gunsmiths and steel cutters, known for their precision and design skill.

Generations of them had lived in the valley beyond Mission Ridge and many had worked for the city's stove-making industries—there were three big companies in those early days—when American steel was produced in abundance. Except for an errant uncle, the modern-day Peters clan was a solemn and temperate lot, circumspect in their dealings.

As a young girl, she understood the family's way of doing things, but had an innate curiosity the others had either suppressed or lost. Influenced mostly by her father, she was always drawing. The two of them would plan projects together that ranged from birdhouses to barns. The most memorable one being a rabbit hutch with three levels and an elaborate latching system to protect them from predators.

In high school, she took drafting classes. When she discovered that a distant cousin worked as an architect in Los Angeles, she contacted him. That connection to the profession allowed Maddie to observe the work, get good advice on education and later, it provided her internships with prominent firms working on major structures, including the extraordinary J. Paul Getty Museum at the Getty Center in Brentwood.

She learned to work with other creative individuals, was straightforward with her peers, quick to sense opportunity and exceptionally hardworking. The family had expected her to pursue a career in business, so when she chose to study architecture, they seemed stunned.

Eventually, Maddie's father supported her decision, believing she had a vision for the future. Her father knew that the city's steel days were numbered, whether for stove works or wheel bearings, so he had entertained the idea of the family starting a new business. Maddie could be helpful in that. But she was determined.

Her father's intuition was confirmed when one of the

city's largest industries, United Steel and Foundry, failed, creating rings of bankruptcies among builders and their subcontractors. The steel crash changed the face of the city and, in some ways, provided Maddie with the opportunities that helped her make her name in architecture.

The classic education of architecture included a spectrum of cultural exposure—art and design, textiles and dyes, travel and cuisine. Maddie soaked it in like a dry sponge. The more she learned, the more she wanted to know. She was visually creative and unafraid of the challenges presented, first by her instructors, and later by her clients.

She also displayed a talent for handling complicated projects and working with all types of people while keeping calm under pressure. When she launched her firm, she realized that it might be a more difficult career path than she had imagined. Early on, requests for proposals were hard to win. In fact, she was plainly told that it was ridiculous for a woman to even attempt to compete with established firms. It took a long time to get the work. But she began to win projects and later became one of only two, approved state historic architects.

When Joseph Kronenberg joined the firm, he added focus and more elaborate business strategies to her artistic mix, helping to ground the company and generate growth. The team she put together was stronger and more assertive than ever.

The first government contract finally came through in an expansive program of updates to technical community colleges through the State Board of Regents.

The Bowers Firm completed inspired projects on time and within budget. The building community respected them and could find, well—not so much to criticize.

Personally, Maddie had the respect of her employees, contractors, and subcontractors. Her biggest problem was getting developers to understand her vision for their properties. This compelled her to find those who were creative collaborators, not those who were interested in predictable formula work.

Although not always cooperative, builders were eager to see what she would come up with next for her unusual array of clients. She dreamed of starting a construction arm of the company, something her family might even understand. The work Maddie did was beautiful, and her timing was impeccable too. The company caught the first swell of growth in the nineties and eventually rode the wave of progress into a new century.

At first, she focused on nothing but developing her business. The possibility of a romantic relationship had not entered her mind. When she first encountered Russell on campus after an American Institute of Architects workshop, he was a tantalizing diversion with a sunny disposition and a blue-eyed gaze that made her forget to eat the bowl of Tom Yum she had ordered. Where did *he* come from?

The attraction was immediate and mutual. He had her number before he left the Global Village Café that day. They were married six months later at a chapel on a nearby mountain, beginning a successful collaboration of intellects, talents, and passions. He was sensitive and observant, good at noticing the minute changes in the demeanor of people around him. That quality made him helpful to his students and brilliant as a husband.

Maddie was direct, but not conventional. She was always looking for imaginative ways to solve design problems. Not always able to express her emotions verbally, she felt her way along in the world, pouring herself into the next project as she grew the firm.

Not surprisingly, she found that Russell had a deep interest in historic properties and often would pursue research that was helpful for the firm as it took on the renovation and repurposing of existing buildings. While she sourced the modern materials and subcontractors, he left nothing to the imagination, providing detailed reports on the original architects and builders, their suppliers and construction crews. He tracked down the information on how the buildings were used and when they went into decline. Their relationship was amenable in so many ways.

Starting a family was not high on their list of goals, yet when their first child was born the following year, they were unexpectedly delighted. The baby boy was named Nicholas Arthur, after Maddie's grandfather. How could anything so pink and wrinkled be so fascinating?

Even later, when their daughter Merritt was born, they were reeling with excitement. The children's first words and initial steps were recorded and celebrated. Baptisms and birthdays were photographed in detail. The magnet school they attended was part of the city's revitalization, with plenty to offer the children in the neighborhood.

Nick went off to a big city university in the north to study business. He had worked over the summer as a paid intern for a logistics company. Now at the end of the season, he was coming home for a break before beginning the fall semester and Maddie looked forward to his arrival days before her housewarming party. Only Nick didn't know about the house, and she was apprehensive about his reaction.

Merritt wouldn't be home for two more weeks. She may have been trying to avoid confrontation at home, since her International Studies coursework, although colorful, did not promise gainful employment. Russell had been trying to get her to think about a degree in education. In his own way, Russell was as blindly dedicated to his field as Maddie's family had been. To have not one, but *two* children who weren't interested in teaching almost broke his heart.

That night Maddie picked up Nick, who came in on the last flight from New York, looking sleepy and already bored. The small airport had added several direct flights and although it was far more animated than it once was, the rotunda was hushed.

"How was your flight?" Maddie asked.

"Crowded, and I'm starving."

When Maddie made the turn up the Ridge, he perked up. They turned into the driveway and stopped in front of the massive house.

"Whose house?" Nick grumbled. "Look, could we just go home?"

"Well, you *are* home," Maddie said. Russell came trotting down the broad steps of the old mansion. It took a few minutes to put it together.

"What? No way. I never thought you'd sell our house," Nick said when he stepped into the oversized foyer of the house on Mission Ridge, his eyes taking in the chandelier and paneling.

"It was perfect, and all my friends lived in the neighborhood," he grumbled as he lugged his suitcase up the stairs. But the lavish space of his new bedroom, officially the guest suite, quelled his complaints temporarily. When he energetically bounded down the stairs an hour later asking where the minibar was, Maddie knew he was on board.

After a few days, living in the old mansion seemed perfectly normal. It would be a great place for entertaining and everyone looked forward to the upcoming soiree.

CHAPTER ELEVEN

1890
Chan Yee

THE MANCHU CONQUEST of the Ming Dynasty and over two hundred years of related upheaval had led hundreds of thousands of refugees to resettle in Quanzhou, a port city on the southern Malay Peninsula. The city lay between the estuaries of the river Jin and the river Luo, where they flowed into the Quanzhou Bay on the Taiwan Strait. Chan Yee, like most of the refugee population of Quanzhou—called Straits Chinese—was English-educated. Like many from the Chinese diaspora in the nineteenth century, his services were sold by labor recruiters.

The Chinese were sought after for their work ethic. However, most of them were unskilled and their terms of indenture were long. If the workers survived their heavy labor—often that depended on where they were sent—few of them had enough money to return to China.

The unluckiest had been sent to Cuba during the 1870s, where they were immediately diverted to quarantine stations to be stripped of clothing, their queues cut. Most of these men were then sold directly to the sugar plantations. After years of twenty-hour days, poor food, and worse treatment, most were never seen again.

In the end, almost all Chinese workmen found themselves far from home and impoverished, their health depleted by the end of their service.

It would be tiresome for Chan Yee to list all the outrages against the Chinese he had seen and heard about over the years. He had experienced the racism firsthand, yet he had been healthy, hardworking, and fortunate. Fulfilling his five-year obligation on the completion of the wall, he had arranged to marry a young girl from his hometown in China, sending money for her passage.

Her name was Yu Yan, and she wore her shining hair pulled back into a knot at the nape of her neck. The corners of her soft mouth turned up and her eyes were kind. He took out a tattered photo of her and gazed at it whenever he became restless or worried. She was courageous, and her image offered hope.

She arrived just before the passage of the Chinese Exclusion Act. She sent Chan Yee letters from New Orleans, where she was living with her uncle's family and taking care of a young girl from a wealthy family. The girl would go to boarding school next year and Yu Yan would join Chan Yee in the spring. He would travel to the Chinese community in New Orleans by train and finally bring her home.

Chan Yee knew he had been lucky up to this point. He liked the city; its humid climate and hilly landscape reminded him of home. His laundry business was doing well. He took particular pride in his ability to remember his customers' names and their preferences. His prices were fair, and the city was growing.

But now, after burying Sam and Ida, he wasn't so sure.

Chan Yee was determined to find out what had happened to the Wahs. That determination overrode his caution, and he visited the police precinct the day after the funeral. No one would talk to him about the hangings, and he was sent away. He went to the newspaper office and talked to a reporter who had first reported the story. The reporter, Martin Walker, said that the Cameron Hill society woman had overdosed on laudanum and the Wahs had been seen leaving her home. Her husband was enraged and grief-stricken.

"Reason enough, according to Chief Ottinger, that a small mob would form and take retribution," said the reporter. "Yet no one admitted to anything, and the storm washed away any trace of the culprits."

When Chan Yee went back to the precinct, Ottinger again alluded to the drugs. "Everybody knew they were involved in illicit activities," hissed Ottinger. "It was just a matter of time before they got caught."

"It is unlawful to hang people without a trial," Chan Yee said, careful to keep a calm demeanor.

"Well, course it is," said Ottinger. "But listen, we got no clues as to who did it. There are no witnesses, except for that traveling salesman that saw them leave the house. The woman's husband wasn't even around—he was seen sitting in a bar most of the night. All we know is what the papers reported, right here on page one," he said, thrusting a copy of the *Daily News* into Chan Yee's hands.

On the way home, Chan Yee reread the account of the lynching and noticed a few other articles he had missed before.

The Daily Times, July 27, 1890
Lynching Follows the Death of Society Woman

On the morning of July 25, the bodies of Sam Wah and his wife, Ida Wah, were discovered by residents hanging from the crossbeams of the recently opened County Bridge, here in the city. They were pronounced dead by the city coroner, Mr. Josiah Wallace, at nine o'clock.

An itinerant seller of brushes, Mr. Ramsey Durant, told authorities he saw the pair leaving from the home of Mrs. Margaret Montaigne, 432 Cameron Circle, on the evening of July 24, around seven o'clock. He gave detailed descriptions of the couple and the wagon in which they left the home, where she was later found dead in her front parlor.

The deceased, Mrs. Montaigne was the wife of Henry Montaigne, Vice President of the First National Bank. She was involved in many charitable drives and organizational events throughout the community. Mr. and Mrs. Montaigne were influential in the recent neighborhood anti-crime league awareness campaign to clean up the lower city, near the riverfront. Family members report that Mr. Montaigne is overcome by grief for his deceased wife and is not available for comment.

Police Chief James Ottinger was quoted saying, "We have no information about this lynching except that the Chinaman, Sam Wah, was seen leaving the premises and was in possession of a great deal of opium." The lynching on the new bridge, which makes the northern reaches of the county accessible, happened only days after its opening. Lead bridge engineer, Edwin Thatcher, had no comment except to say that he didn't think the incident would have any impact on traffic across the bridge.

A severe storm coincided with the violence of the evening of July 24, when lightning started several fires around the city and many trees were blown down. Officials have reported that all evidence of the hanging may have been washed away by the storm.

Mrs. Montaigne will be laid to rest in the Forest Hills Cemetery on July 27, after a two o'clock memorial service at the Church of the Good Shepherd.

June 1887
Beehive Fire Commemorated at the New Fountain Plaza

The ninth day of June last year was a typical summer day for the men of the City Fire

Department's Lookout Company, until four o'clock when they received the alarm that would forever change their lives. It sounded from Box 25, the new Standard Gas Machine and Economizer, adjacent to Beehive General Store at the corner of Fourth and Market Streets.

Chief Whiteside was in command at the time and firefighters Henry Iler and William Peak responded, arriving in only minutes to lay a line at the rear of the store. According to eyewitnesses on the scene, just after they got there an explosion of great magnitude occurred and a storm of red-hot bricks rained down on the men. Henry Iler was completely buried and was said to have been killed instantly. Officer Peak was buried to his shoulders and died later that night, leaving behind his young bride of only six weeks.

Local businessmen donated money to kick off a relief fund for the families and devise a plan to memorialize the sacrifice of these two brave men. "It has been suggested that as a monument, a large fountain be erected in a public place, surmounted by a life-size sculpture of a fireman with a nozzle in his hand from which a stream of water is flowing," said the chief. "Given by our fellow citizens, we will memorialize our heroic fellow firefighters, and mark this grim tragedy.

"For long years into the future we will pay homage to the firemen of the city," said Chief Whiteside. "To those who are willing and ready to risk their

lives to save the lives and property of the city's residents."

Chan Yee refolded the paper, thoughtfully. There would be no justice for Sam and Ida, he knew. Maybe no peace for their souls either. Rumors swirled around the incident for weeks, including everything from robbery to sexual assault, before being pushed to the background by the dedication of the fireman's memorial and yet another news story of a warehouse fire at the docks.

Almost three months later, on a Wednesday morning, Chan Yee noticed Dr. McNallie at a newsstand on Main Street. The doctor was said to have treated the Montaigne woman for nervous disorders with his patented medicine. *Wouldn't he have some insight into her death?*

Chan Yee walked over, said good morning, and introduced himself as a friend of the Wahs. Startled, the surgeon grimaced.

"I have wanted to speak to you about them for some time," Chan Yee said. "They would not have done any of the things people say they have done. It must have been someone else, or possibly an accident. Was she not your patient? What do you think happened?"

"Your friends and their crimes have nothing to do with me," said McNallie with a snarl. "If you speak to me again, I'll have you arrested." He threw down the newspaper he was about to buy and hurried up the street through the slush of a late snow.

○ ○ ○

A few days later at the laundry, Chan Yee looked up as a small man entered the shop and dropped a bag onto the counter. "I'll pick up these items on Tuesday for Dr. McNallie," the butler told Chan Yee. The butler had brought the fine winter coats to be cleaned at Chan Yee's laundry.

"Certainly," Chan Yee said as he folded the heavy woolen overcoat and velvet cloak, placing them in a cart. He handed the butler a ticket.

Chan Yee knew of the surgeon's fondness for luxury. He had observed that Dr. McNallie wore handsomely crafted boots and carried a cane with a knob of silver. His wife ordered beautiful silk from New York and Milan for dresses she had sewn from a catalog of styles by the best seamstress in Nashville. They had the finest carriages and, in the years to come, would have the fastest roadster in the entire county.

The house on Mission Ridge was one of the first with electric lights and a few years later, a refrigerator in the kitchen. There was a maid, a cook, and a groundskeeper on staff to keep everything running smoothly. The cook always procured the freshest vegetables and meats, serving the food on hand-painted China.

When spring of 1891 came, the surgeon's pasty-faced sons were learning to play tennis at the only court in the city. Their mother had costumes made for them so they would look stylish, and, although they had no aptitude for the sport and there were no other children playing at the time, they reluctantly appeared at the court twice weekly until the heat became oppressive.

That was also the spring when Chan Yee boarded the train to New Orleans for the journey to bring Yu Yan home. He closed the shop, making sure to deliver any clothing to his customers and carefully placed a sign on his door stating that he would return in four or five days.

Chan Ock would feed and water the chickens he kept in the small patch of yard behind the laundry.

He pulled on his coat, gathered up a small packsack, donned his Fedora, and headed for Central Station. Control of the Alabama Great Southern Railroad Company operating out of the city had just been sold to the Southern Railway and train travel was on the rise. Flocks of travelers gathered on the platform to wait for the morning train. The scene flattened in the mist — a panorama in black and gray. He bought a round-trip ticket for himself and return passage for Yu Yan.

The morning sun was burning through the fog when the last whistle blew. Chan Yee found a seat in the rear car and settled himself as the train lurched and pulled out of the station. It rumbled through a tunnel or two before finding its customary speed. Then, through forest and farmland the steam engine hurtled deep into Alabama, stopping only in Birmingham and Tuscaloosa. Only half full when it left the city, it slowly picked up individuals and families from the state's vast rural counties that were headed to the big port city on the Gulf of Mexico.

The flat land of the piedmont opened on either side and the newly planted and plowed corn and cotton fields were as wide as the day was long. He lunched on the rice cakes and hardboiled eggs he had stowed in his pack. He dozed. With brief stops in Jackson and Hattiesburg, they picked up more rural passengers. They boarded the train in waves. Women with infants, men in working clothes, even vendors with cages of chickens and rabbits. As the train neared New Orleans, the stops became more frequent, calling attention to names he did not recognize — Slidell, Pearl River — until finally the destination was achieved.

When the train stopped it was overflowing with all manner of colorful folk, all with various dealings and pursuits to address in the bustling city of New Orleans.

Chan Yee made his way to the house of Wang Li Yong at 226 Liberty Street in the Third Ward, after staying overnight in the Chinese Rooming House on Tulane Avenue. Along the way he passed the many markets that had opened near the Chinese Mission, where at the beginning of the decade, a Boston missionary named Lena Saunders had begun teaching English, American culture, and Christianity to the Chinese populace. It was becoming an important force in the community. Yu Yan had described vividly the activities of the teachers, students, and the general community she encountered as she was studying English at the Mission in her letters to Chan Yee.

Why, you would never think anything could stop them. So many clever people have started businesses—opening shops on every corner, offering novelties of food and apparel from home.

The Mission helped make the Third Ward neighborhood around South Liberty the geographical hub of their community. New Chinese-owned businesses were launched in a patchwork pattern here. They became the core of the first and largest Chinatown in the Southern States.

There was so much activity and energy in the neighborhood, Chan Yee felt giddy. He almost walked past the unassuming two-story Victorian house, except that its bright red door and Chinese letters on the postbox drew his attention.

The narrow walkway to the front step of the tall, gray house was welcoming enough. Yet his excitement was for this evening when he would be married. Yu Yan was waiting for him behind the red door. Her uncle Wang Li

Yong, his wife and his sister had engaged the minister of the Canal Street Presbyterian Church to marry the couple in the parlor of the house. The service would be followed by a simple tea ceremony arranged by the women. The tea ceremony would honor Yu Yan's aunt and uncle for all they had done for her.

By seven in the evening, when the sun was low, a select few guests began to arrive, ready to see the service. They had grown fond of Yu Yan and were eager to see her enter the room as a bride and greet her betrothed.

The bride was dressed in a plum-colored silk qipao with deep red trim. Richly embroidered with gold thread at the collar and cuffs, it had belonged to her grandmother.

The wedding guests included two of Yu Yan's fellow English students from the mission, one of whom was an accomplished player of the Bawu, a side-blown free reed pipe. The night was warm and the breezes from the open windows carried the instrument's rich melodies onto the air, softening the transition from the western marriage vows to the beautiful tea ceremony.

The rhythm of the ceremony was hypnotic to Chan Yee. He watched Yu Yan's long graceful fingers as she poured the tea for her aunt and uncle. He saw moments of his former life in China. He let the memories wash over him, carried by the music on the breeze. That night in the upstairs bedroom, the ache in his soul was soothed.

Yu Yan

Yu Yan and her new husband enjoyed the food and friendship for days. Walking in the fascinating streets of the French Quarter, shopping in the Chinese neighborhood and generally getting to know each other better was invigorating. The time was well-spent and when Yu Yan had said her many goodbyes, the couple boarded an early morning train for the long trip home.

Yu Yan's aunt had packed a box of culinary delights from the local shops as well as her own creations from old family recipes. Some had been used for hundreds of years. Dishes made with noodles, rice, cucumbers, and bean curd had been served for four thousand years. At least that's what her aunt said, and her aunt seemed to know everything.

Though her possessions were originally modest, her friends had been generous in their gift giving. So many things—decorative chopsticks, jade beads, hand-carved wooden ducks. Yu Yan was overwhelmed. They decided to ship some of the items, including a small, lacquered chest holding a tea set and several richly embroidered blankets, even though it might take months for it to arrive at home. Time was theirs she believed, and she planned to use it.

The trip down had seemed long and solitary, but the way home was dappled with sunlight and seemed to pass more quickly, according to her new husband. From the window, the mid-day heat blurred the late spring landscape. Passengers boarding in Tuscaloosa climbed onto the train and by the time it stopped in Birmingham, it was filled to a steamy capacity. It was exciting to see so much more of the countryside and such a variety of people riding the train.

Eventually, she became drowsy.

Chan Yee

So many people were going in different directions. Chan Yee watched as two nuns helped a blind girl disembark and check for the address of the doctor she was to see. People reunited with their families. Some set off on journeys into the countryside.

Those leaving the train car were immediately replaced by new passengers. Chan Yee stood up to let a mother with a baby take his seat. From there, he observed through the window the passengers boarding the car ahead of them and recognized a man from the city, although not one of his customers. Just then, the train shuddered and lurched forward. Yu Yan's rattan suitcase fell from the upper storage rack, its lack of square corners causing it to roll instead of stack on the cramped shelf. Chan Yee caught the bag and, after rearranging the luggage, restored it to a space on the rack. When he straightened, the man could no longer be seen. Passengers boarded and got off, until they found better seats and were finally comfortable.

After a light supper of rice cakes, the couple dozed. Chan Yee's eyelids fluttered, and he dreamed he could hear the voice of his friend Sam Wah, calling from a distance. The voice was calm, but insistent. He seemed to be working on the wall again and Sam was very far down the line, calling for him to come. He turned to go toward Sam, but the closer he got, the further away Sam seemed to be standing. His frustration was rising. Again, he walked toward Sam, until he was running toward him, but never reaching him. Then he felt the tracks beneath the train rise like a slow tide. He opened his eyes and remembered. It took a moment to calm himself as he looked at Yu Yan. Her eyes were closed.

Chan Yee reached over to take his new wife's hand and gave it a gentle squeeze. Her presence alone gave him a sense of satisfaction and confidence he had never known. When she stirred, he gave her a moment before speaking.

"How do you feel about the way the ceremony turned out?" he asked, curiously.

"I thought it was lovely. My friends all said so," she said, eyes glistening. "So many wonderful blessings. Yet now, I'm looking forward to my new life with you." She smiled the beautiful smile.

"I hope you will like it. There is plenty to learn with so many new customers. The city is growing so quickly," he added, surprising himself with his own excitement.

It was dusk when the train pulled into Central Station, but the evening was pleasant. He was happy to show her the streets of the city. Talking quietly, they walked four blocks to Eighth Street and took a shortcut through the alleyway toward the laundry on Sixth.

Passing O'Dell's tavern at the corner of Sixth and Broad, he saw the passenger from the train through the window, sitting at the bar, and now he remembered—the man was a downtown banker. Henry Montaigne, the husband of the dead woman.

"Wait here for a moment," he said softly to Yu Yan, as he stepped inside the tavern, obscured by the coat rack near the entrance. He could hear the drunken voice of the banker, "I put a generous jigger into her teacup, that's all."

"And that's what the chink and his wench got strung up for?" asked O'Dell, the Irish bartender. "What a story."

"They had it coming," Montaigne mumbled and shrugged as though it couldn't be helped. The overhead gaslight chandelier cast deep shadows below the eyes of the men, their reflections warped in the polished wood of the bar.

Breathless, Chan Yee stepped back outside, took his wife's arm, crossed Sixth Street and walked to the modest quarters where he lived above the laundry.

Chan Yee

In the South, each community developed differently, most often carrying on the traditions passed to them by earlier generations. Some towns were mining towns, some river or rail communities, but all were influenced by their own interpretation of faith, or some form of moral compass. Chan Yee couldn't shake the feeling that the city possessed a duplicitous aura of mystery. The confusing stew of religious fervor and racism, polite manners and cruel disadvantage was served up daily.

He knew Yu Yan had questions about the mood of political activities here. Beyond the typical segregation, how were immigrants generally treated? Reluctantly, Chan Yee considered how much he should reveal. When he finally told her the story of the hanging, she was disturbed, yet she encouraged him to continue to try to understand what had happened. And since he now believed Margaret Montaigne's husband was responsible for her death, he should go to the police with the information.

Police Chief Ottinger had been in charge of bringing criminals to justice for just under sixteen years. He had been hand-picked from a rather large group of candidates after the former chief, a popular and progressive thinker with a knack for detection, accepted a sudden and unusually attractive job offer in Nashville.

Ottinger's ginger-colored handlebar mustache and silver sideburns seemed to give him a stamp of wisdom and the illusion of integrity in his position, although he did what he was told by the influential men of the city, without question. After the War Between the States, the city's oldest law firm had actively advertised in the North for carpetbaggers who would come down and seize control of resources that could be used in manufacturing and build new foundries. The foundry capabilities drew many types of manufacturing. New wealth attracted inventors and patentholders, beverage, candy and bakery pioneers, makers of metal wheel parts—even penniless publishers. They came for a time, built great fortunes, and it was to these men and their heirs that he owed his allegiance, not so much the law or the voting public.

As long as the city was growing in the way they wanted it to, there would be no problem. But if someone became too powerful too quickly, he might suddenly be under investigation for certain criminal acts. Mysterious fires at the dock warehouses might victimize the newest manufacturer to compete with the establishment.

Power was a delirious commodity that belonged only to a chosen few and greed was the wall that kept the unwanted on the outside.

When Chan Yee had questioned Ottinger's lack of interest in justice for his friends, his own lack of prudence endangered him. No matter, one sunny morning he decided to share what he knew. First, he told Chan Ock, who didn't seem surprised.

"You need to let it go. You have to think of Yu Yan," he said. "Don't spoil everything now, after you've waited so long to bring her home." Chan Ock didn't know whether to be fearful or dismissive. His friend's kindness and his intellect had always shown through his demeanor and had often kept him from being the object of abuse. But he was being stubborn about this.

Chan Ock had the notion of bringing his own wife and daughter, now living in New York City, to be with him. If Chan Yee caused trouble that might not be possible. Staying in the city at all might be risky.

Chan Yee did not let it go. Later the same day, he took

the trolley to the precinct office. He sat in the back in the segregated section where four black men in work clothes and two women with shoeless children sat. These horse-drawn, segregated streetcars would become a symbol of the Jim Crow laws, almost as much as the poll taxes levied against ethnic groups and poor whites. Just a few years earlier, a Black man named Charlie Williams shot a street-car driver who tried to enforce the city's segregated seating ordinance. Williams was lynched at the jailhouse the same night. Twenty years later, Blacks would boycott the streetcars of all three lines operating in the city. However, attorney Styles Hutchens, one of only two Black men sent to the Tennessee General Assembly from the county, was at least successful in repealing the poll tax for the city in 1888.

Chan Yee got off the trolley at the end of the block. He walked up the street to the low brick building, entered, and asked for the chief. Perspiration collected at the back of his neck, dampening his starched white collar. He had to try one more time.

Ottinger grimaced. Chan Yee knew he was not pleased to see to see him there, standing with hat in hand, waiting at the end of the hallway. Ottinger walked the length of it, shaking his head.

"Chief Ottinger, I have some information for you about the death of Margaret Montaigne," said Chan Yee. "I overheard her husband tell the barman on Sixth Street, that he had given her the medicine himself."

"That case is closed," replied Ottinger. "And anyway, nothing is going to bring your friends back now." He could show sympathy for the loss, but he didn't want the Celestial stirring this thing up again. Before he could say anything else the man was spouting some obscure Chinese philosophy.

"Without wisdom we cannot become persons of virtue, without fidelity we cannot be authentic," added Chan Yee under his breath. Yet, he knew virtue was the last thing on Ottinger's mind.

"Look, you have a family now—a wife. I'd be careful if I were you," said Chief Ottinger with a raised brow. "If Henry Montaigne or the surgeon find out you're still causing trouble, they could make things nearly impossible for you."

Chan Yee looked at the red faced, blue-eyed man who could hide behind a row of large white teeth better than anyone he knew. He had to accept that the events of last summer would never be completely revealed to him. The life he and Yu Yan would build for the future had to begin now.

Yu Yan

Yu Yan was excited for the success of her husband's business. She was learning about the laundry, getting to know the customers, and was trying to avoid thinking about the rich cultural community she had left behind in New Orleans. She missed her aunt, her circle of friends and all their social activities.

"You just need to make some new friends," Chan Yee said one day as he noticed her staring out the window, wistfully.

Encounters with the women of the city made her uncomfortable. Their eyes would sweep down her dress and back up again as she walked along the street or shopped in the open-air market on Eighth Street. But she didn't look away. Their eyes met her steady gaze when, as they looked up again, often were even greeted by a thin smile which seemed to unnerve them. Her qipao was well made of quality fabric, but unadorned, befitting her station in Chinese society. They would simply have to get used to her physical presentation, she thought, since she was not quite ready to wear western clothing.

She came from a family which followed Confucianism. When mixed with religion, philosophy, governance, and tradition it could be complicated. But, in its simplest form it could be described merely as the way of living. Confucianism held one in contempt for failure to uphold the cardinal virtues of Ren and Yi. Ren was benevolence, or the essence of human compassion. Yi was the moral disposition to do good. To be compassionate and do good. These were the values she attempted to hold and observe.

Yu Yan's Confucianism transcended the tension between religion and humanism by considering the ordinary activities of human life, especially relationships, sacred. Social harmony was emphasized above other spiritual values. The worldly concern of its tenants rested on the belief that human beings are fundamentally good, improvable, and perfectible. Oddly, she thought the teachings of the Canal Street Presbyterian Church were not incompatible with the values she was taught as a child. Social justice and harmony ranked high with the Presbyterians, as well.

She missed the congregation and was anxious to stay in touch with its activities and the general well-being of her friends there. When the postman came bearing a letter from her aunt, she was thrilled.

July 22, 1891

Dear Yu Yan,

Now that you have gone to your new life, the house here on Liberty Street seems so quiet. I have always felt happy about the name of my street, and we do have many liberties, yet this society imposes many boundaries. Some we see, others are invisible. It is confusing that the states are all so different in their interpretation of the law.

Our cousin Hong Yen Chang is so smart, and a gifted young man. He graduated two years ago from the Columbia Law School, but he did not have United States citizenship. Last year, he was granted both citizenship and the right to practice law in New York. This was useless since when he moved west to practice in San Francisco he was not allowed to do so because of the horrible Exclusion Act. We were so disappointed for him! He is such a fine-looking man and always wears western clothes.

However, Hong Yen has appealed the decision denying him a license to practice in California. He expects it to go all the way to the Supreme Court. We are hopeful that he might win his case and be allowed a license. He might even be the only Chinese American citizen to practice law in this country.

How is your handsome husband? I hope his business is prosperous. We look forward to hearing news of you. Please write soon.

Blessings,
Mae Lin Yong

August 16, 1891

Dear Aunt Mae,

I was grateful to receive your letter, since I have been missing you and my old friends. We sometimes feel so far away from home. Fortunately, my husband's associate has a wife and daughter who have come to join him here. Now that there are two other Chinese women in the city, it will be less lonely.

I hope that Hong Yen Chang's appeal will be successful. It seems that he has worked so hard. There is always plenty of work, isn't there? To work diligently and not be recognized or compensated for it is unjust. Yet, the faces of exclusion are many. The faces surround us and stop us in the path. Our Baba used to say, "There is no greater calamity than being consumed by greed." It is true. It fuels all manner of trouble and chaos, causes so much pain and suffering.

I knew Chan Yee was a kind and generous man, but now I am so pleased to observe that he lets these troubles roll away. He is determined to expand his business and is opening another laundry across town that Chan Ock and his wife will operate. The shop will be on the South Broad side of town. Chan Yee believes the area will grow. He is always so hopeful. We are fortunate, and if he can let his troubles roll away, I will do the same.

I am considering buying a pair of shoes. It could be a good way to begin to build a wardrobe of American clothing. In the laundry business you see all the new styles! Although it may take some time, I am optimistic.

Write soon, Auntie, and tell me the news of all my friends. Be well and may your happiness flow like the endless waters of the sea.

Yu Yan

Chapter Twelve

1995

Russell

THE DAY OF the party, the sky was clear with the promise of a stunning sunset. An events company spent the day setting up magnolia-laden tables on the lawn around the sculpture of a ten-foot abstract great blue heron, a frog held captive in his mouth.

The caterer brought trays and baskets, laying the long butcher's table that served the open kitchen with fresh vegetable cones, grilled okra and corn, mounds of shrimp, beef empanadas and pastry puffs. Enormous platters of barbeque sliders were carried out to the veranda by black-clad college students who would be hoping for sizable tips from the hosts at the end of the evening.

The veranda was full of ferns and potted gardenias that were beginning to bloom, their dizzying perfume heavy on the evening air. The ringing of cicadas in the woods nearby reached a soaring pitch.

Lizzer and Zach helped the musicians set up on a stone dais at the back of the lawn, where a temporary dance floor had been laid over 140 square-feet of recently re-leveled flagstones. As the lights in the east valley began to twinkle, the band started with classic Beatles songs, clearly their specialty. They had specific repertoires for almost every occasion and had several names for the band, quartet or ensemble, as need demanded. There were eight, four or three musicians. When playing a wedding they were Bubbles & Strings. When a rock concert was called for on the Fourth of July, they were the legendary Eight Knives, and for an evening event such as this one, they were simply Nocturne, a string quartet which began with British pop music and morphed throughout the night.

The finale music would be both powerful and peaceful when heard with the water cascading from the nearby fountain. This iteration of the group was often reliably described as "energetic, yet mysterious."

Guests began arriving almost before Russell was out of the shower. He quickly threw on a blue-checkered shirt with his white trousers, and headed out to greet them. The neighbors from two doors up the street had walked down and were the first to comment on the improvements at the old house.

"The widow had let things go a bit too long," said Cynthia Simons, a hospital administrator. "You have it looking beautiful once again—and I love what you've done to the sunroom!"

"Well, thank you, we're working on it," said Maddie, exchanging a smile with Russell. "Feel free to wander around the downstairs rooms, Cynthia. Those are the only ones we've had time to renovate."

Zee arrived dressed in white from head to toe, and Russell made her a unique pistachio cocktail. Always trying to impress the people he especially liked. Some noticed, others did not. Zee, who always noticed, smiled gratefully.

"It's my take on a Manhattan," Russell said, handing her the green cocktail. "I call it the Sicilian. Let me know how you like it."

Marvella arrived with a guest in tow, a violinist she met in Gdansk last summer who was here on a performance tour. She was dressed in a short emerald tunic made of silk, her long legs glittering beneath it and ending in jewel-blue stiletto heels. Blue-and-green feathers adorned her spiked red hair.

"Maddie," Marvella said in her patented breathy, pan-European accent. "You've done a fantastic job with the renovation. What an extravagant beauty this place is."

Marvella's gifts of enthusiasm, optimism and a generally rich sense of humor were magnetic. She was loyal and helpful—a natural promoter with wonderful connections who could get the word out about award-winning projects and accomplishments. Incredibly, she seemed to have time for everyone.

She stood with a couple of other working artists clustered around. Her husband was a mosaic artist who lived in Spain and worked on colossal projects for the resort industry around the world. He rarely traveled for any other reason. On the other hand, Marvella traveled for every reason and had chosen a house on Mission Ridge as her summer residence. She had a nose for potential patrons and soon began chatting with Cynthia.

University friends and volunteers for the local preservation organization, Cornerstones, had come to see the work-in-progress. Across the lawn, they were in an animated conversation with Maddie about the intricacies of saving historic residences.

Another cluster of guests followed Russell across the grounds as he expounded on what was left of the roses at the west side of the house. He was thrilled to show off the rose garden created by one of the former owners, a city mayor, even if he'd had nothing to do with it. The mayor's sister, the widow, had been the master gardener. He could picture her here in her simple cotton housedress and sunhat, walking down the long row of thorny brambles reaching higher than her head. Heirloom roses, most of them, in every color. Their fragrance was intoxicating during the height of the season. There were several amateur rose growers among the group and the discussion about the comeback of Heritage rose varieties soon left Russell's informal history presentation by the wayside.

"Russell," said one of the neighbors, "you've got to speak at the next meeting of the local chapter of the Rose Society!"

"Oh, no," Russell said amiably. "I'm no gardener, just a fan. But I might attend some of the meetings, I have so much to learn. By reestablishing the garden, I want to create a showplace for the community." By the time Russell concluded the tour, the rose growers were thrilled, and they scattered in small bands, chattering enthusiastically and occasionally bumping into pockets of artists and craftsmen.

Among the guests was Ray Bowman, a Melungeon man and wood turner who displayed his exquisite work in the Cliffside Gallery on the bluff. Bowman's family went back for centuries, descendants of the European settlers of the Cumberland Gap, African slaves, and Cherokee people from North Carolina. His craft was ancient and although he was reclusive, he seemed to value his association with Maddie and her network of friends. They offered him opinions, contacts, and a cadre of enthusiastic customers. Suddenly, the voice of Isaac the sculptor boomed across the yard.

"Where is my favorite patron?" he bellowed.

"Everyone loves it, Isaac," Maddie declared, appearing at his side and gesturing to the fountain. "It's the best part of the renovation."

Isaac was a large man in all senses, dressed in a yellow Hawaiian shirt. Alongside Maddie in her ruby cocktail dress, the pair resembled a hummingbird at a column of jasmine. By the time the sun cast low bars of gold across the ridge, the back lawn was full of garrulous people—laughing and enjoying what was turning out to be a magnificent evening.

As shadows began to deepen, a stooped figure quickly crossed the lawn and blended into the scene. Who had invited Dr. Bowers? Many may have wondered had they not been deep in conversation and well into their third drink.

What Russell could remember of his brother when they were boys was vague, at best. But some things were well documented. Graydon Bowers had attended the best prep school in the city and then went on to undergraduate studies and medical school at Vanderbilt University. He had come from a family of educators and often complained loudly that they were stodgy and critical—his father and two aloof uncles. They never took him seriously.

Russell had to admit, their father was frequently off to conferences or speaking engagements wherever the American Association of Educators was meeting. Professor Gordon Bowers was not particularly interested in discourse with either of his children, but he had seemed particularly disappointed with Gray. Consequently, his older brother was always slinking off, dissecting some small animal he had captured. He got excited when torturing mice or amputating frog's legs to see how long they could live without limbs. After he finished, he enjoyed burning the refuse in a bin on the back lawn.

He was completely disinterested in history, often citing one of Henry Ford's less thoughtful quotes, "The only history that is worth a tinker's damn is the history that we make today." This loosely adapted remark had been picked up from a well-meaning seventh grade science teacher.

Russell remembered that when Gray was unable to get what he wanted or confronted and held accountable for his own mistakes or weaknesses, he responded with brief, violent outbursts unleashed on anyone nearby. His family contained the situation because they were able to draw on their vast connections in education and the community at large. A fight at his private school, cheating on an important exam or the simple avoidance of rules–all could be made to go away. And if the family's reputation would be jeopardized, it did go away. They found it disgusting, however, and he knew he was disliked by his own. He would show them. He would be the first surgeon among them and would someday get their attention.

The field of cosmetic surgery was a fledgling one in the city with fewer practitioners than in Atlanta or Nashville. Russell thought his brother's actual talent might not have been as great as his ego, or he might have gone elsewhere. He seemed to prefer to be the bigger fish in the smaller pond. Admittedly, he was the highest-rated plastic surgeon in town. All went well to him in the early years, until he botched a breast augmentation performed on a teenage girl. Her parents sued him for a sizeable amount, but his license was not suspended.

He had married a wealthy young woman from Nashville during his residency, and after twenty-eight years of marriage, she divorced him and took as much as she could, including the house and his favorite car. He seemed more cynical with each passing year and his face had begun to tell the story.

Russell knew his brother resented him and thought his wife unconventional. He could tell he was envious of the house, too. The way Gray saw it, his pathetic kid brother had married poorly, achieved less and through dumb luck, was happy and popular. Russell felt his condescension, keenly.

Gray

Gray's discovery of the house was quite accidental. Two years ago, he had dropped by the estate sale the widow and her son conducted as they were clearing out the contents to ready the house for sale. The upkeep had become more than she could manage, and her son had established roots in Greenville. She would move there to be near him in an assisted living facility. Sadly, or maybe not, she died in her sleep the week before the move.

It was a mild spring day and Gray had nowhere to be. He pulled up and parked under the shade of a tree at the foot of the hill. He walked up the drive among a reasonably good crowd of curious browsers. The veranda was cluttered with items retrieved, from attic to basement, that had collected over the past ninety-seven years and four previous owners. An assortment of chairs and small tables. Brass lanterns and light fixtures. Boxes of mismatched dinnerware. Teapots, jewelry, and books on many subjects.

Gray casually shuffled through a couple of boxes until he came across a thin, bound volume of indeterminant color. Many of its yellowed pages fused together in sections. The title was "On Top of the City" and it was a history of the house written by the original owner himself—who coincidentally happened to share his profession. He became intrigued by an old photo of the surgeon and his family standing near the house with the wall extending up the roadway near the top of the ridge. There was a newspaper clipping about the opening of his clinic, too. In the same box there were even a few ledger books with patients' names and medical records. He paid five dollars for the entire box and took it home to examine. What he found amid the dust and clutter that day was surely meant for him. In fact, the house itself would have been his if they had not interfered. He took his time reading the articles about the way the house had evolved. He found diaries and notebooks that brought the reader into the twentieth century.

During prohibition in the 1920s, after the death of the surgeon and later his widow, Edward Morrison Finnigan, the owner of the city's biggest restaurant and only speakeasy, bought the home. Dressed in a fine suit and a Homburg hat, he unlocked the door for the first time with great pomp. His wife felt the mansion was fitting for them and since it was her family's money they had spent–she had made the choice. He went along with it, although he would have liked to be closer to the club, known simply as Finnigan's. His business dealings, however, reflected his own unique choices. He wasn't sure his wife shared his preferences.

At Finnigan's downtown establishment, the right kind of customer was escorted into a blind alley behind the restaurant's kitchen. He provided a password through a sliding window in an unmarked door and was allowed entry. The establishment served attorneys and judges, manufacturers, and contractors, even a few government officials. Secrets were Finnigan's specialty, and his customers paid well for the privilege of being insiders.

His wife was always nervous about her husband's business and not entirely comfortable in the house. She chronically complained of her pantry being reorganized while she was gone. The canned goods would be moved to a higher shelf and stacked alphabetically. She soon found herself eating at the restaurant more and more, buying fewer items from the local grocer.

Gray continued reading until an article about the mayor appeared. The article, along with a few international news items seemed to forecast a gathering storm.

Times were changing and the newspaper headlines reflected both new resolutions and a growing instability in the world. In 1933, the twenty-first amendment passed, making the control of alcohol a state issue instead of a federal one. Prohibition had officially ended. Then in 1939, Hitler invaded Poland and the second World War began.

Finnigan had just sold the house to the new mayor, E.D. Bass, a man who was born in the city and had come from humble beginnings. Dedicated to civic duty, he took the reins of his responsibilities and never looked back.

Mayor Bass was so busy during this period that the house on Mission Ridge was hardly more than a place to sleep and being a widower, he rarely entertained. But the housekeeper complained frequently that the basement door wouldn't latch and was always open. She had the latch removed and a hook placed on the door. She would hook it, but later it would be open again. She quit soon after and was not replaced.

Bass thought the house was just too much for him and to waste the fine home on a single man seemed poor stewardship. He considered selling it, but when his sister's husband died unexpectedly, he asked her and her young son to come and live there. He would retire to an apartment at the back of the house. They accepted his offer.

The delighted nephew roamed the woods and open spaces that would become the sites of important battlefield monuments. The sister loved gardening and spent her time cultivating a spectacular rose garden. She didn't care about the interior of the house at all.

Her collection of old-fashioned roses that included Madame Hardy and Mister Lincoln, first introduced in the mid-1800s, was the talk of the garden club.

When her brother retired, she plunged even deeper into the pastime. Experimenting with the Belle of Portugal, a flesh-pink climber introduced in 1903 that grew prolifically in California, she expanded the style of the garden. A hybrid tea rose called the Charlotte Armstrong, introduced in 1941, took Garden Club awards every year after she added the variety. She added other varieties like Lavender Lassie and the Queen Elizabeth rose from the 1950s, as well as a collection of English Shrub roses that debuted in the early 1980s. These were the last additions to the rose garden. The widow never remarried and after the death of her brother–the city's bold mayor– she lived there until her own peaceful death at ninety-four. *Gray read the entire account of the history of the mansion on the ridge.*

Bonnet

Now, Bonnet the terrier had a mind of her own and it was singular in purpose. She knew what she knew and would not let it go. The thing had to do with a persistent smell, an irresistible adventure that urgently needed attending. She had been in the kitchen's large pantry since the party began, and after first scratching franticly, had settled at the top of the basement stairs at the door. There she could inhale deep drafts of stale air subtly laced with the mysterious emanation.

Oh, there were plenty of other things to sniff, with all those noisy people around, but she could not let go of the attraction that kept her at the door of the stairs. Suddenly, her opportunity came in the form of a server looking for an oversized tray which was hanging on the wall just inside the doorway to the basement. Her moment had arrived, and she made a quick dive down the stairs without anyone noticing. In his haste, the server pushed the door almost closed, but not latched.

"How like them to have a party to show off their conquest over me," Gray muttered to himself as he quietly crossed the street that night. He entered from the west lawn and slipped onto the veranda, unnoticed. Shadows of the guests danced in purple hues along the lawn, and garden lights swayed in a faint breeze above their heads. Someone was prattling about his recent fishing trip to the Bahamas—bone fishing in warm aquamarine waters with his college chums, drinking rum at an upscale fish camp and telling stories until well past midnight.

Dr. Bowers slipped in through the kitchen door, unseen. He passed the sink where two servers were working, deep in serious conversation about whether one should move in with her boyfriend, a lawn maintenance laborer with a gambling habit. He crossed the length of the room, past the island countertop with its burden of stacked plates and a bin of used glassware. Into the butler's pantry to the top of the stairs. The door was, of course, open. The dark recess of the basement then swallowed him up, completely.

Maggie noticed Bonnet sitting in the grass a couple of feet away with something glimmering in the light, dangling from her mouth. She called to the dog and Bonnet reluctantly walked over and dropped the object in front of her. It was a slender bottle with something dark inside. Maddie reached down to pick it up. Typically, the dog changed her mind, snatching the bottle in her mouth and with the agility of her breed, dodging the legs of guests, leaping over pot and around post, sped off toward the kitchen door. Maddie quickly pursued the dog. Up the steps, across the veranda, through the door. She passed the students, hurrying to finish up so they could go for a beer.

At that point, the evening changed. The temperature dropped by two degrees and a cool breeze from the west blew in, enough to make the garden lights sway and their reflection shimmer in the pool below the fountain. The crowd mellowed, too, as though lowering its collective voice.

It may be reliably said that the closest thing to magic in the modern era is coincidence. Maddie caught sight of Bonnet's tail disappearing down the stairway to the basement.

Pausing only briefly at the doorway, Maddie slipped onto the dimly lit steps and went down, waiting at the bottom to let her eyes adjust to the low light. She could hear a scraping sound coming from the room. In fact, the second door was open, and light poured from the once hidden doorway — the recesses of which had been created due to the surface of the ridge rolling off somewhat on the southwest corner.

In contrast to the relaxed scene of the garden party outside, the lower chamber was tense, the air stagnant. Bonnet was barking with urgency. Maddie began to cough.

The sight that met her at the door was surreal. There was Gray, dressed like a cat burglar, shovel in hand, his wavy silver hair forming a ridiculous halo around his head. The wan light from the electric bulb cast dark shadows under his eyes when he looked up at her. In the hole, hundreds of small glass bottles had been unearthed, many already stashed in a canvas bag nearby on the dirt floor.

"Gray? What are you doing?" Maddie called out incredulously, raising her voice to be heard over the barking dog.

Ignoring her entirely, Gray tossed another handful of bottles into the bag and kept digging. However, Bonnet had reached her limit— she grabbed the bag in her mouth, ran over to Maddie and dropped it at her feet. Maddie bent down to pick it up and as she stood up, she glimpsed the shadow of the shovel coming down on the side of her head and top of her shoulder, knocking her to the ground. She lay stunned for a moment, then backed away frantically across the dirt floor, screaming. "Are you crazy?" Rolling to one side, she got herself upright. Her ears were ringing loudly now, and her mouth and nose felt hot and wet.

"This is mine," he roared and started toward her. "You didn't even know it was here—you don't know anything." Maddie turned and ran for the stairs. She scrambled halfway up before she felt her head being yanked back. He had a fistful of her hair, and she was being pulled backward. She tried to pull away. Suddenly, they both lost their footing on the crumbling masonry, somersaulting to the hard-packed dirt floor. Maddie felt a sharp pain in her side and pushed away from where she had fallen on the shovel lying in the dirt. She struggled to breathe.

Just then, a man stepped into the shaft of light from the open door above. He was slender and elegant, wearing a white shirt with black trousers, and he stood over them on the landing. There was something ethereal about him. His Asian face was a study in concern as he looked down on the chaos below. Was it concern or disdain?

Gray, stunned by the fall, tried to focus on the apparition. That face. Slowly, a hint of terror entered his eyes. He knew this man, had read all about the times the surgeon had seen him over the years, especially near the pantry. He was the Celestial, the storekeeper. He had read the accounts of his comings and goings—up the steps of the basement or carrying brown boxes down into the basement. Stocking the pantry shelves.

The surgeon's fevered accounts of the specter had filled the pages of his diary, kept during the last days of his life. The very diary that Gray Bowers had scoured for information once he realized in astonishment that a treasure of laudanum was buried in the basement of the Mission Ridge house. The panic the surgeon felt had compelled him to dig a hole late one night and bury the boxes so there would be no immediate proof of any involvement in the overdose of Margaret Montaigne. The police chief and the others complicit in the murders might tell, and he wanted no lingering evidence to connect him to her death or to the hangings.

Suddenly, a wave of vertigo swept over Gray and his disorientation was overwhelming. When he looked up again, he saw a young Black woman standing next to the man. And then, perhaps the most pathetic of all, there appeared the woman he knew as the whisperer, who was said to have whispered by the mantle clock with her eyes closed.

"Maddie?" called the man on the ledge. Rising up on one elbow, Maddie recognized the violinist, Robert Yee. "Uh, I was just looking for the restroom. I heard someone coughing and the dog was barking. Are you all right?"

Yee was standing there alone, of course, to everyone but Gray who, perspiring heavily, rolled over and vomited up his rage along with the veal cutlet he'd had for dinner. Maddie looked at him in the dark room the way you look at something familiar and, for the first time, see it the way it truly is. She hadn't read the diary and she didn't know what was going on in his head, but she would come to know all of it. She began to cough again.

By the time one of the students fetched Russell to the basement, Gray was sitting sheepishly on the steps. His stupor suggested a head injury and Maddie had a brutal headache from the blow of the shovel.

When Russell saw Maddie, bleeding from her nose and mouth he grabbed his brother by the shirt. He dragged him up from where he was sitting in the dirt. In a wave of uncharacteristic rage, he looked into Gray's vacant eyes. "You sad piece of shit." Then he punched him.

They called an ambulance. Police Sergeant Billy Howell also got the call and directed by the students, found the scene in the basement. After methodical and lengthy questioning, and Maddie's description of the attack, they agreed to categorize the incident as domestic violence—the biggest problem in the city. Technically, it was domestic, after all.

Gray Bowers felt a connection with the surgeon, and a fascination for the diary, especially the reference to the laudanum in the basement. Who knew if it was even still viable after nearly one hundred years? It didn't matter.

Maddie later dropped the assault charge and Gray spent three months in a court-imposed drug rehabilitation facility. The family's attorney suggested he continue his counseling for one year. Russell was naturally hopeful, but Maddie was skeptical.

"I know Gray seems contrite now, but old habits die hard," said Maddie. "And, I don't like the look in his eyes." She put away the last of the serving trays used at the party.

"Well, there isn't much we can do about it except try and have a little faith in him. He is getting professional care."

"Yes, but I'm not sure I have that much faith."

"Faith is the bird that feels the light when dawn is still dark," said Russell as he leaned in to steal a kiss. "According to my favorite Indian philosopher."

"How mystical," she said with a smile. His optimism actually *did* make her feel better.

Maddie and Russell had strong, though not entirely typical feelings about the way everything had happened. After all, Russell believed life was not a series of random events, but rather an expression of a deeper order. Events that led to the insight that a person was embedded in a universal wholeness were more than just intellectual exercises. They were elements of a spiritual awakening, not only potentially for Gray, but for them as well. A meaningful coincidence could only be explained by a phenomenon of energy. Perhaps an energy that had long awaited articulation.

When Maddie greeted Zee Lunsford at the kitchen door the following week, she asked about how Gray was responding to therapy. Zee's response was reserved yet hopeful.

"He may never exactly be lighthearted, but I think he'll achieve some kind of harmony." While it was difficult to muster anything resembling affection for him, Maddie and Russell were somewhat relieved. Yet, Maddie would never forget the malicious attack he had inflicted on her.

In an effort to change the subject, Maddie began to talk about the house. Zee was curious about all the upgrades. She had watched the work crews coming and going. Since the party, a few more deliveries had been made for new installations. They shared their plans for completing the renovation of the old house, along with some observations about a transformation they had noticed. For Maddie, the house was alive and not just with its ghosts.

After the evening of the party, the house above the Wall almost sighed with relief. She knew it in her soul. For her, the apprehension of the previous months melted away and she sensed an unexpected lightness. Instead of dreading the return home each evening, she felt welcomed, even consoled by the house.

Russell was aware of it, too. He had been drawn to the structure for its classic design, the long history it possessed and the mystery he felt surrounding it. Although now its mood seemed less malevolent, more peaceful.

Somehow it even seemed more physically appealing, the colors warmer and brighter, luminous at times. The house was suddenly open to allowing the inhabitant a capacious and luxurious expanse in which to breathe. Its accommodation was almost extravagant. Maddie turned her considerable talents toward the continuation of last summer's remodel.

After the roof, many renovations, both subtle and pronounced would eliminate the shadows and bleach the dark wooden surfaces, so the interior would be bright and inspiring. New windows would replace the ancient ones. Modern bath innovations would create a spa-like retreat in the master suite. New lighting would enhance the indoor living spaces, and dramatic lighting for the patios and porches would create a magical evening experience that few would forget.

Outdoors, new tunnel arbors were to be established. leading to a completely revitalized rose garden in a tribute to the most satisfied former resident—the gardener. Russell had arranged for new varieties to be planted by the local garden club and classic Heritage roses would continue to be cultivated in every color so that the garden would be the highlight of the neighborhood renaissance. His strategy was to open it for tours in the summer to raise money for the local historic preservation organization, part of a plan to underwrite the cost of saving and improving its new project, the old train station.

Even before the party, they had the photograph of the Chinese builders Vivienne had discovered reproduced and enlarged, matted, and framed with museum-quality materials, then placed in the foyer of the house. *A place in time.* It would be the focal point for sharing history and entertaining guests. It would become a daily reminder of the transient nature of life. The wall the Chinese immigrants had built on the ridge would become not a statement of social distinction, but an enduring complement to the old home. The past was present in the wall and implicit in the future of the neighborhood.

So, on the night of the party when most of the guests had gone, including the police, only Robert Yee was left standing in the foyer staring up at the oversized print of the Chinese construction crew. Maddie and Russell had been saying their goodbyes. Finally, the perplexed Robert looked at them and asked a question.

"I've been wondering . . . why do you have a picture of my great grandfather on your wall?"

They were stunned.

"My grandmother has a photo like this in her family album." He pointed to Chan Yee in the image of the group. "That's him."

In the following years Maddie and Russell would enjoy long afternoons in the shade of the veranda. House guests and extended family would share the beauty of Hunt's architecture and the fine craftsmanship and solid building techniques used by Chan Yee, Sam Wah and their coworkers. Secrets had been unearthed. Time had recognized the anonymous, and if there were ghosts, all were resting, and no one spoke in a whisper anymore.

CHAPTER THIRTEEN

1891
Chan Yee

CHAN YEE AND his friends were excited to hear about a new hospital that would soon be built, providing more options for all people and the surgeon was not involved, they noted with relief. An out-of-town investor had provided a grant for a new medical facility. As with most progressive things that happened, it had come about because of the railroad.

A German financier and Parisian banker, Baron Emile d' Erlanger, who had railroad investments in the city had donated a huge sum to build the first permanent regional hospital. His holdings included railroads and mines in Africa, North America, South America, and Europe, as well as Russian and Tunisian government bonds and Southern cotton, during the American Civil War. In the late 1870s, Erlanger invested in the British-owned enterprise, which eventually funded the takeover of the Alabama Great Southern Railway. It also included the Cincinnati, New Orleans, and Texas Pacific lines. This railroad network, known as the Erlanger System, was around eleven-hundred-miles-long at the time.

Fundraising continued as the hospital acquired four acres on East Third Street. Administrative staff, doctors and nurses were then hired for the new facility, the finest in the region. Chan Yee attended the cornerstone celebration for the seventy-two-bed hospital, where he stood on the periphery of a large crowd. Families had turned out in record numbers for the event.

The decision was made to name the new facility after the Baron's wife, a Southern-born woman from Louisiana, Baroness Marguerite Mathilde Slidell d' Erlanger.

Without any connection to the new staff, the surgeon was completely out of touch. The house above the wall was a tribute to his skill, intelligence, and hard work. However, it was a dwelling place, not a monument. It was a quiet place now, he and his wife no longer entertained as they once did. His power in the city was more assumed than real. A medical society had been established to raise money to provide care for the indigent, but no one asked his advice or sought his counsel on the future of local medical care. His general dissatisfaction left a sour taste in his mouth.

After getting their education, his sons began to practice medicine in the valley with the same, bland, lack of compassion. They began raising their children to harbor inflated expectations. All of them felt the same insatiable hunger for wealth and attention.

Perhaps the entitlement the family felt was due to an exaggerated sense of being set aside for greatness, for no apparent reason. To be first in line—always. They were sanctified for "leadership," which had become a code word for their greed. The surgeon's dark soul was a yawning breach in the landscape of compassion. Chan Yee had heard about sanctification through the scriptures, yet he had his own ideas about that.

"Sanctity is an empty cup," Chan Yee said to his friends one night over a dinner of rice congee and smoked river perch. Chan Ock's wife and daughter had finally arrived and the small group was celebrating.

"It's like a beautiful chalice that holds nothing. Only when filled with the wine of kindness does it become worthy and accessible." His friends only nodded and, although his eloquence was noted, it changed nothing.

"Kindness is not exactly what we experience in this new place, is it?" said Yu Yan. They ate in silence until the daughter told an amusing story about their trip.

"Why *do* they dislike us so?" Yu Yan asked Chan Yee later that evening when they were alone. Do they hate us only because we look different than them? Chan Yee was thinking about the clothing he saw each day in the laundry.

"This kind of hate is just greed in another costume," he said. "We are not just different. They are worried that we are different and we might *get* more. More power, more opportunity." He paused to sort these thoughts, finally sighing. "This life is full of complications."

It annoyed him that he still wondered. He felt sure the surgeon was somehow responsible for his own patient's death and maybe even the deaths of his friends. But there was nothing he could do, no justice for the powerless.

Chan Yee's Buddhist mother had been deeply influenced by Kwan Yin, the Buddhist bodhisattva known as the embodiment of compassion. To Buddhists, it is she who hears the cries of the world. His mother had often talked of the cycle of rebirth—and the unfortunate realm of ghosts and hell that all want to avoid. He wished he could talk to her now. No matter what became of the surgeon in life, Chan Yee knew that when he died, the realm of ghosts was his to inherit. Maybe the ghosts were with him already.

It was clear to him that the world of the living could be filled with apparitions and hellish nightmares. But if that was true, then heaven was also present among the living.

He watched his friends and saw their potential. As he looked at Yu Yan with feelings of affection, longing and hope—he knew the complications of living did not outweigh her beauty and love. Her industrious nature was a jewel to her community. She hoped, she persevered.

He and Yu Yan would go on living in the city, expanding their business and opening three more laundries in other parts of town. Eventually they moved to a house on a corner lot in a nearby neighborhood. They would raise a family. Their children would graduate from university with honors and afterward, they would become teachers and professors. As is often the situation, the children would take their parents' fortitude for granted, yet would gradually become extraordinary citizens themselves.

The Surgeon and the Specters

Future owners would realize the house above the wall had its secrets, as all vintage places do. Pull away the vines, and there were hidden doors; open doors and there were winding staircases. Loose bricks hid childhood treasures tucked away in moments of guileless intrigue. Dark spaces concealed more clandestine activities.

It was after his retirement when the surgeon began to really inhabit his impressive home on the ridge. He became aware that he was not alone. He would see movements at the edge of his peripheral vision. At first, he dismissed it as the result of a chronic drinking habit. Although when he drank less, the sensation of shadowy movement around him only seemed to get worse.

Not long after his children had left the home, he would awake from dreams, sweating and shaking. Sometimes he heard noises when he wasn't asleep. Then he would go downstairs to have a look around, walking the hallways, starting at shadows.

One night, the surgeon saw a woman standing outside the parlor window looking in at him. Or she would have been looking, but her eyes were closed. Her lips moved as if to speak, but all he could hear were muted whispers. He saw her again on another evening, standing before the clock on the mantle, whispering to herself. The whispering increased. He could hear it in the daylight hours, out in the garden and inside at the foot of the stairs.

If she had been the only apparition he saw, he might have come to terms with the image. But there were others–a small dark woman, whose sadness was deep and palpable. She carried a garment in one hand and shears in the other. And of course, the elegant man in the white shirt who appeared when least expected, his anger smoldering like embers. He knew who they were.

His wife could not see the apparitions, but she went to great lengths to placate her husband, suggesting that his health was in jeopardy, he was working too hard. She brewed herbal teas. She made compresses of eucalyptus and lavender. After weeks of disturbed sleep, she traveled with him to Hot Springs for a month-long treatment for his nerves.

Chan Yee saw the couple at the train station as they were leaving. He said hello, but the surgeon's eyes were blank, without recognition, and he was mumbling as he passed by.

Nothing seemed to help. As time went by, he became more and more reclusive. He began to write down each sighting in the pages of his own diary of the great house on the Ridge. The secrets of the house were there, along with detailed accounts of the sights and sounds from those fear-charged nights and exhausted days. He became sure of one thing—while he couldn't always heal the sick, he could raise the dead—just by being in the house. He often sat in his chair near the fireplace and became completely accustomed to the comings and goings of the specters.

Then one day Chan Yee read in the paper that the surgeon had died. The detailed article said he was found in the parlor sitting in his chair. What the story didn't mention was the mantle clock striking the hour of his death. Oddly, the clock kept sounding but never moved beyond that hour. The maid took it to the clockmaker to have it repaired.

The funeral arrangements were meant to be elaborate, but the energy went out of the family. Chan Yee went to the graveside service and stood at the back of the small gathering. They buried him beneath an oversized marble monument in the Forest Hills Cemetery with the factory owners, bankers, and lawyers. It rained during the graveside service which was completely unadorned and poorly attended.

Chan Yee

Chan Yee met Yu Yan at the door to relieve her of some of the bags she was carrying. He gently pushed a twig of her hair back behind her ear before he took them. She seemed so tired lately. After one year, the second location of the laundry was thriving, they had hired another worker and there was no need for her to do so much. But when he mentioned it, she often shushed him and said, "I like to work!"

Today she was grateful for the help and by the time she had cooked the rice, made his favorite spicy sauce, placed the pickled eggs and duck on the table, she was thankful for a chair. Tonight, she wanted everything to be perfect. The food was excellent and although the days were still warm, the clear nights had cooled off considerably. She surprised him with a decanter of plum wine and after supper they sat on the porch gazing at the stars.

He was expounding on what a wonderful day it had been. He had stopped to see an old friend. The business was growing. The price of heating oil was down below last year. She reached over and took his hand and drew it to her lips.

"My love, I'm going to have a baby. We're going to have a child," she almost whispered the words. So softly.

"What? I thought you said . . ." A shiver went through him. "A baby?'

He was overwhelmed by the news and for a moment his ability to call up English words was impaired. All he could utter was "Kai Xin," meaning joyous, happy.

They slept in each other's arms that night and Yu Yan dreamed of a beautiful meadow filled with wildflowers. She began picking them and the more she picked, the more sprang up to take their place. For her, the feeling of abundance in life had been rare and she awoke thinking it was extremely pleasurable.

Months later, Chan Yee and Yu Yan strolled along the

path above the river. The sky was blue with only a few puffy white clouds gliding across the sky. Below, rowboats were pushing their way across to the North Shore and a rough landing dock beneath the bridge.

They were discussing names for the infant who would soon arrive. Yu Yan's name meant beautiful smile, which was nice. But if a boy was born, Chan Yee did not want his child to be named after him. They still had some time to think about it.

"A western name would probably be best."

They heard a cry in the distance and felt the pathway pounding. As they looked up, they saw Chan Ock running toward them. He jogged up the path, smiling and waving something in his hand. When he stopped he said, "The postman was at the gate and he left this for you, Yu Yan."

"Oh, thank you," she chuckled at his enthusiasm. "It's a letter from Auntie Mae." She read it quickly and was animated by the news. Her eyes shone as she reached for Chan Yee's arm.

"They are coming in one month to visit and be here for the birth," said Yu Yan. A sense of relief tinged with only a bit of apprehension came over Chan Yee. He cherished his wife and wanted her to be looked after. Her aunt would make her feel secure.

"That's wonderful."

"Oh, now there is even more to do," she said as she turned toward home. He smiled and gently took her arm.

They had been planning the move for some time. The house on the corner was bigger than any they had dreamed, and they had barely moved into it when Wang Li Yong and Mae Lin arrived. Bustling with treasures from New Orleans the visitors filled the kitchen with special treats and the spare room with mysterious packages.

Yu Yan was large and uncomfortable, yet she was intrigued by the beautifully wrapped presents. It was all they could do to keep her out of them, since it was unlucky to open them before the birth. There would be plenty of time afterward anyway, during her month of confinement.

She was tired of waiting, and had only a few friends to talk to. One day Mary Lou Adams, from her church congregation, stopped by to pay a visit. Aunt Mae brought them a cup of tea.

"You look good," she reassured Yu Yan. "I brought you something."

Yu Yan looked surprised.

"You never got to meet her, but Ida Wah was an amazing seamstress and she made this fancy handkerchief. She gave me two of them at her wedding," said Mary Lou. "I want you to have this one." Delicate lace edged the square of fine silk. Inlays of pale blue fabric formed a relief for the embroidered image of yellow and purple wildflowers in a meadow, blue sky overhead.

"Just like in my dream," Yu Yan said. "Why, thank you, Mrs. Adams."

"Well, I hope all your dreams are as pretty as that."

That evening Yu Yan's labor began, and although tradition often dictated that men leave the house while the midwife and attendants delivered the child, Chan Yee waited in agony in the outer room, listening to the cries of his sweet wife while their infant son was born. They called to him and he ran into the room, hair disheveled and shirtsleeves flying. He kissed a smiling Yu Yan and a small, squirming bundle was thrust into his arms.

Quietly, he moved to the window, gently swaying back and forth. The stars were shining brightly and the moon had risen high above the horizon.

When he spoke, the baby stopped and listened. "How

frail you look for this world," he said in amazement and gave it a mental shrug. "You will grow."

Four weeks later, Yu Yan and her infant joined Chan Yee at a full moon party for their son. The relatives and friends were there for the celebration. A table was laid in the center of the room. Yu Yan made the table look like a meadow full of wildflowers, with grasses and flowers rising from low trays of green moss, filling the center runner on the blue cloth. Plates, bowls, chopsticks and flatware lined the edge of the table, so that everyone might be seated. The sideboard was laden with red eggs and ginger, rice and skewers of crisp duck.

Wine was poured, and passed, and poured again. Many of the guests offered blessings and brought gifts. It came time for the baby to be presented and Chan Yee raised him up in front of everyone and said, "I would like for you all to meet our son, Sam."

There were soft comments of approval and a toast to the spirit of the first Sam and many more to the new baby and his parents.

Author's Note

The Inner Wall is a work of fiction. While the wall in the story represents economic, cultural, and spiritual boundaries, there is no physical wall.

The Chinese characters were real, and I discovered them through the research of the local Historical Society. They were not hanged, however, and much of their story has been obscured by time.

The New Revised Standard Version of the Bible, used for Reverend Thirkill's sermon was not actually available in 1890, but I thought it was the clearest option for today's readers.

While many of the characters and incidents in the book are historic, any similarity to modern persons is coincidental.

Acknowledgments

In this novel, I draw from a twenty-five-year career as a writer and editor for city and environmental magazines. Thanks to all of you who were kind enough to collaborate.

Thank you, Anna Sutton of Raleigh, North Carolina and BookLogix of Alpharetta, Georgia for reading the manuscript and helping with some of the structure across multiple timelines.

I would also like to thank my son-in-law, Brian Chan, for complaining that Asian men are rarely considered for romantic leading men roles in our stories today. It inspired me to share Chan Yee's story.

Most of all, thanks to my husband, John, for his patience and helpful suggestions.

9 781665 308212